Beyond the Pale

Also by Laurie Brady and published by Ginninderra Press

Slices

Pursuit

Rummy

Rapport

Laurie Brady

Beyond the Pale

Beyond the Pale

'Pale' was the name given in the fifteenth century to that part of Ireland that had been colonised in the twelfth century by Henry 11. It was only in these districts of Ireland that English law prevailed. By the sixteenth century, the English Pale was confined to a small area about twenty miles around Dublin. The expression 'beyond the pale' has undergone a generalisation in meaning to refer to behaviours that are not necessarily outside the law but are patently unfair, or outside the limits of social convention.

Beyond the Pale
ISBN 978 1 76041 733 8
Copyright © text Laurie Brady 2019
Cover photo: David Marcu via Stocksnap

First published 2019 by
GINNINDERRA PRESS
PO Box 3461 Port Adelaide 5015
www.ginninderrapress.com.au

Contents

A Question of Motive

'You can't park here, sir.' The young constable approached the car with a torch and peered in the window, then, suspecting Ed's identity, asked him his name.

Ed paled visibly, even in the rotating red light flashing on top of one of the three police cars parked outside his house. One had turned into his driveway and its high-beam lights illuminated the front yard and entrance.

'What's happened?' Ed whispered breathlessly, unable to move from the driver's seat.

The constable looked at him sympathetically.

'What's happened!' Ed shouted, finding his voice as the realisation dawned that something terrible had occurred, and fearing the worst, he wrestled with the door handle. 'Tell me! For God's sake, tell me,' and opening the door, he stumbled and fell onto the road, where he sat and rocked backwards and forwards, his head in his hands. 'Don't tell me it's Lucy. No, it can't be. You can't tell me that. No, no,' he babbled.

'If you give me the keys, sir, I'll park your car over near the kerb.' The young constable, who barely looked as if he'd begun to shave, didn't need an answer now to his question, and was trying to do what his training had taught him.

'It is, isn't it? It's Lucy,' he whimpered. The significant police presence confirmed it, though he had been too shocked till now to ask for details. 'Is she, is she…?' He grasped the constable's arm and looked at him pleadingly, as though his mere intensity might change an awful reality.

The constable eased the keys from his grasp, and moved to the driver's door. 'If I could ask you to stay right where you are, sir. Sergeant Wakeley will be with you right away.'

Ed knew his worst fears were well grounded. There wouldn't be so many police otherwise. He was still sitting on the road. A procession of police, some sheathed in white protective gowns and footwear, entered and left by the brilliantly lit front door. It seemed like a pantomime. Perhaps it was simply shock that had shut down his senses. Neighbours in several front yards, some with their children, watched silently from the shadows, still in their pyjamas.

'It is Mr Stanlake, isn't it?' A voice reached him from some subterranean depth. 'Sergeant Wakeley. Keith Wakeley.'

Ed looked up to see a beefy man with the bare arms of a wrestler, and bushy eyebrows. The Christian name was added as a personal touch to inspire confidence.

'Is it…?' Ed queried.

'Yes, I'm afraid it is. I'm sorry. I can see you're in shock, but if you feel able to answer a few questions now, only a few, we can do the rest tomorrow.'

'But what? I mean, was it…?' Ed knew the answer. An accident would not bring this number of police, and suicide was out of the question.

'Yes, I'm afraid it was,' Wakeley pre-empted. 'The coroner and a forensic team are in there now. I'm not at liberty to give you details yet until the cause of death is established. And we'll need you later to identify the body. Not that there's much doubt. She was still in possession of a driver's licence and credit cards are in her wallet, and the pictures on the dresser…'

'But was she…and how…?' Ed's mind was chaotic, running in all directions.

'It's unlikely that she was raped. Now, I think you'd better let me do my job and ask the questions,' Wakeley assumed his official role, though not without sensitivity, and helped Ed to his feet.

The questions concerned Ed's whereabouts that night, his time of departure, and his knowledge of his wife's movements. He asked about any recent conflicts and unusual phone calls, and there were a couple of veiled questions about the happiness of their marriage.

'We'll be here most of the night, I'm afraid. Is there anywhere you can stay? Is there someone you'd like the constable to call?'

'I'll be all right,' Ed answered, not by any means certain that he would be. 'The neighbours are kind.'

As Wakeley hurried away to be swamped by the attentions of other officers reporting on the tasks they'd been given, Ed felt light-headed and, suddenly aware of the sour taste in his mouth, was sick in the gutter.

The house was only fifty metres away, lit like a beacon, and Lucy was sprawled inside. Would he ever be able to return there? Were her eyes open, revealing the terror of her final moments? Was there much blood? Was she disfigured? For the first time, the images flooded Ed's mind. Was she decent? That would be so important for her.

'Ed.' It was Lois Channing from next door, a coat over her pyjamas, shivering from emotion rather than cold. She hugged him tightly as if the need were as much hers as his. The tears were rolling down her cheeks. 'You can't go back in there. You're staying with us...for as long as you like.'

*

It wasn't the usual television interview where the bereft partner begs the public for information, choking back tears and appealing to the murderer to do the right thing. There were no tears, though Ed did speak haltingly of his love for Lucy, and left it to Wakeley to make the usual appeals to the public. He didn't want the interview, believing his relationship with Lucy didn't need to be publicly affirmed. He thought the overt and extravagant show of emotion even cheapened what they had. Still have, he kept telling himself.

But Wakeley thought it might help, and television news programs were thirsty for coverage. A puzzling murder of an attractive woman in one of the better suburbs, and one that carried the possibility of being a crime of passion, was enticing television fare.

The public was sympathetic to Ed, though a few, given to egregious displays in television viewing, believed he might have displayed a great deal more emotion when interviewed.

The press gave commiserating coverage, showing photographs of the house, and a stylish one of Lucy taken at a conference a few years earlier. It provided a sanitised account of the murder scene, and described Ed's background that, to his displeasure, had been provided by a once-close friend.

His days at school were reported, revealing him as a good student, perhaps something of a loner, and fond of intellectual pursuits rather than the usual rough and tumble of boys' games. He'd been out with a few girls, but his first real girlfriend was Lucy, who he'd met in his first year out of school.

Growing up wasn't that easy for him, one paper reported, and, with great poetic licence, related the story of his brother Billy.

When Ed was nine and Billy was seven, the family had taken their summer holidays at Forster. The boys' father had gone out in a boat fishing with a mate, and their mother went shopping, telling the boys she wouldn't be long, and insisting that they stay in the holiday house till she returned. Look after your brother, she'd told Ed. But the lure of the nearby beach had been too compelling, and the boys decided to take a quick swim, a swim from which Billy would never return.

Ed retained visions of the pale thin body, so unvintaged, pulled from the surf, the closed eyes as though he were sleeping. It remained a clinging picture of innocence and purity. Ed never forgave himself, the newspaper reported. Can we possibly imagine, the writer continued, exploiting the sentimental.

The father left a few months later, leaving Ed alone with his mother, but things were never the same. And neither was she.

Another paper gave a neighbour's appraisal of Ed as 'a bit quiet but a real good bloke'. Lucy was described as a very pleasant woman, one who 'always had a cheery hello for me'. The neighbour insisted on her picture being taken, and was determined that her name be spelt correctly. 'It's Daphne, D-a-p-h-n-e.' Her picture wasn't printed. The words were.

*

Wakeley sat in his office with his feet on the desk, twisting a rubber band around his fingers as he read the autopsy report. A single cut from left to right with a serrated knife that had severed the carotid artery. Definitely a right-handed murderer. No bruises or abrasions. No apparent struggle that probably suggested the victim had been approached from behind. That was consistent with the position of the body. No recent sexual activity. No surprises. The time of death was between ten p.m. and eleven p.m.

'Did you find the knife, Bill?' he asked the junior constable as he entered to report. Wakeley thought the knife might either have been left at the scene of the crime or dumped nearby. That was the usual pattern, particularly if the murder wasn't premeditated.

'We've been over the house, the grounds, the dumpsters and drains with a fine-tooth comb,' Bill replied. 'Nothing.'

Every neighbour in the street had been interviewed and names recorded for later checks. Some were unnecessarily voluble, wanting to share their opinions, others shirked any involvement and were even resentful of being seen with police at the door. One neighbour thought he'd heard a car driving away around eleven o'clock, but couldn't be certain of the time.

'And Stanlake?' Bill queried.

'Clean as a whistle,' Wakeley replied. 'Poor sod really loved her. We're interviewing her work colleagues. We all know about office romances gone sour.' And he smiled grimly. 'It's only a small firm, so it won't take long.'

'And talking of romances: any truth in the rumour about Billings, the lawyer?'

One of Lucy's work colleagues had come forward, claiming that on two occasions, Billings had collected her from work in his BMW. A neighbour, three doors away, said she saw them in a local coffee shop.

'None at all. Apparently he was helping her with the messy probate on her father's will. He was genuinely upset.'

Wakeley removed his feet from the table, and threw the rubber band into a drawer. 'We need that sort of help, but ninety-nine per cent of the time it's hearsay, or scandal-mongering.'

'You've dismissed the idea that it was a burglary gone wrong?' Bill asked.

'It might have been,' Wakeley conceded. 'But something tells me otherwise. For instance, how did the murderer get in? There's no evidence of a break-in.' He sighed and placed his feet up on the desk once again. 'And then there's the lack of a struggle. Of course she might have been taken by surprise, but I think someone had been there with her for some time. Perhaps the work interviews will turn up something. We'll just keep digging.'

*

He didn't have to tell her he didn't like heights. She could tell from the way he held the edge of the basket at arm's length, even as the hot air balloon ascended. It was an expensive first time away at the Hunter Valley, a little different from the visits to the coffee shops and local cinema. They stayed at the hotel for one night, and had to meet in the foyer at five-thirty a.m. to be taken by bus to an open field in the dawning light, where the balloon was filled with helium, and the wind was constantly monitored.

By the time they took off, the sky was colouring to a deep blue and the air was crisp. A gentle breeze lifted her hair, and her eyes were alight with exhilaration. They watched the open fields and vineyards moving slowly and silently beneath them.

'It's just so beautiful, Ed,' she whispered. 'A wonderful surprise,' and she kissed him in front of the balloonist and the other four passengers.

There were smiles, and someone clapped.

They held each other closely for the rest of the flight, realising that something special was growing between them, surging from the opening crack in carapace's restraint.

Memory is not always volitional. It can creep up, as it kept doing for Ed, though there were times in that first fortnight after the murder that he tried to retrace the development of the relationship from the time he first saw Lucy at the twenty-first of a friend, long-haired and blue-eyed, the girl who seemed to possess some attraction for men and women alike. Why him, he often wondered, the quiet and not prepossessing boy who didn't dance. Is that why she chose him, pulling him to the dance floor, guiding and reassuring, and all the time not letting go of his hand?

Marriage always has its tests as two people learn to negotiate a shared reality. There were the inevitable disappointments as some expectations of the other weren't realised, or when one became self-absorbed and neglected the other. But they were always able to talk things through and laugh, and were fierce defenders of each other against attack from outside.

'Was the marriage happy?' Wakeley had to ask, perhaps a little apologetically.

'Yes,' Ed answered unequivocally, and he'd given the same answer several times since to himself.

Many aspects of a marriage become routine, and sometimes the matt of shared lives needs to be buffed, but he felt sure that Lucy would have given Wakeley the same answer.

Ed now lived in the nearby apartment of a friend who had left for overseas. He just couldn't return to the house. Perhaps never. He would hear the crows from his unfamiliar bed, the mournful lament with its human-sounding fall. Above his head, beyond the ceiling's harsh hypnotic light, the possums scratched to tease his early morning images of Lucy. It was always worse in the mornings.

If he ventured outside, the air seemed to weigh too much, and it was one more day to face an indifferent world, to brave the platitudes from well-meaning friends, and the hollow voices that sounded as if they came from underwater caves.

*

'Guilty. He's bloody guilty! Lois!' Ted Channing yelled. 'Get in here quick. It's on the TV. Stanlake's guilty!'

'I don't believe it.' Lois rushed into the family room carrying a tea towel.

'He's guilty.' The word was growing in stature for Ted as its meaning was realised. 'He's confessed.'

It was the first news item, and lasted for several minutes. Snippets of Ed's first interview after the murder, containing his profession of love for Lucy were shown, as was the earlier glamorous photograph of Lucy. Lois and Ted watched, riveted to the screen.

'Good Lord.' Lois sat down heavily. 'Just think, we had a murderer living with us. He might have cut my throat.'

The interview with Wakeley was shown on every network's news. 'It was sound, methodical police work,' he said, with ill-disguised hubris. 'Yes, he's guilty all right. The evidence is incontrovertible.'

'A familiar story,' one television presenter commented at the end of his network's showing of the brief interview. 'How often is it the partner, and after they have given their sob story and pleaded for the public's help in front of the cameras.'

No doubt there were many in a thousand living rooms across the country arguing that they'd always known.

Wakeley had cause to be pleased. The pieces had fallen into place. There'd been an anonymous tip-off, a male voice, to report seeing a man surreptitiously throwing something wrapped in a rag into a local pond, a few streets from where Stanlake had lived. The caller couldn't be sure who it was, as it was twilight and he was some distance away, but he had the same build as Stanlake. Wakeley took a chance and had divers search the pool near where the sighting occurred. Late in the day, they found the knife. It was the missing one of a set in Stanlake's house and, while smudged, there were sufficient prints. Of course it had to be established that it was the same knife that killed Lucy. The coroner claimed that it could be the same, but he was not willing to say so on oath. It was damning evidence. What reason could there be for Stanlake to wrap a knife in cloth and throw it in a pond? But more was needed.

Given the amount of blood at the murder scene, Wakeley surmised that the murderer's clothes would be blood spattered. That likelihood had been confirmed by the coroner. The house had been thoroughly searched, as had dumpsters and local bushland. Nothing was found.

So Wakeley sent his team to every dry cleaner within a radius of ten kilometres. It was a long shot but the effort was worth taking. A small dry cleaner's, eight kilometres from Stanlake's house, was able to produce a dated docket to clean a shirt, with Stanlake's name, address and signature. There could be little doubt now, particularly as none of the other sixteen dry cleaners had any record of cleaning anything owned by Stanlake. And if he wanted something cleaned, why did he travel eight kilometres, and bypass at least a dozen others to do so?

Wakeley conducted the arrest himself. He thought it a shame, because there was residual pity and he liked the man, but he also remembered what must have been a consummately acted show of grief the night he met him.

Stanlake seemed defeated when presented with the evidence. There could be no retreat now, and when Wakeley asked him a second time if he had murdered his wife, he confessed. Yet despite Wakeley's coaxing, then and in the days that followed, he would give no reason, and confirm no details.

The public reaction was hostile. Most had been convinced by Ed's genuineness, so his deception was doubly hurtful. They felt he had made fools of them. Some politicians called for a reintroduction of the death penalty. Women marched in the streets with slogans to eliminate violence against women.

The press had a field day. One newspaper carried the headline 'Great Acting Before the Final Curtain'. Another, in huge lettering simply said 'Hypocrite', and presented the sketchy details of Ed's upbringing, suggesting links to future deviant behaviour.

'The house'll go for a song,' the local estate agents agreed.

*

The *7.30 Report* opted for more rigorous and balanced reporting, introducing the celebrated psychologis Dr Curtis Snell. 'Doctor, a lot has recently been said about psychopathic killers. I'm referring of course to the Ed Stanlake confession. Can you explain what psychopathy is?'

'Simply put, it's an antisocial personality disorder. Most people see the world in much the same way, but the psychopath sees the world differently and has different notions of right and wrong.'

'And how much of this can be explained physiologically?'

'There is some research that indicates the brain of the psychopath is different. Decreased neural activity has been discovered in the para-limbic regions of the brain, the part that controls inhibition, emotions and moral reasoning.'

'What are some of the symptoms that we, without the training you have, might be able to recognise?'

'It's important to understand that the psychopath, and even the psychopathic killer, is an individual, and there may be marked differences. That said, the most typical sign is a lack of remorse. You may remember that Ted Bundy, who killed over thirty women, not only didn't feel guilt for anything, but he felt sorry for those who did.'

'What other signs are there?'

'They tend to lack empathy, have little regard for anyone else, and they are often quite charming, but manipulative. They are always pervasive liars.'

'Dr Snell, are there any social or home factors that might explain psychopathy?'

'Nothing definitive, though poor parenting may well increase the risk. Of course, while some may have been abused, many come from good families.'

'We've heard a great deal recently about Ed Stanlake. I'm sure you've kept abreast of the news. I understand that you would need more time and opportunity to make a valid diagnosis, but in your expert opinion, is Ed Stanlake a psychopathic killer?'

'As you say, I would need the opportunity to interview him. But there are some superficial pointers. He doesn't seem to exhibit any painful feeling of self-reproach, he has excelled at lying and manipulation, and the way he conducted the murder was reckless. I don't want to be misquoted…but yes, I believe it is probable that he at least has psychopathic tendencies.'

*

'Would you cancel my first appointment Denise, and reschedule?'

Andrew Billings entered the law firm of Duggan and Billings at eight forty-five the morning after the news of Stanlake broke, closed the door, and threw the morning paper on his desk. He'd already digested the latest bombshell.

Instead of sitting down in the high-backed leather chair at his desk, he moved to the windows, and watched the stream of traffic from the tenth floor, and the workers scurrying like ants into the nearby office buildings. The intercom sounded.

'Your coffee, Andrew?'

'Leave it,' he said testily, and moved to his chair, muttering, 'What the hell!' He looked at the newspaper again, shook his head, and threw it in the bin. It can't be some elaborate subterfuge, he thought. Or can it? What is Stanlake playing at? Does he know it's a life sentence?

Perplexed, he sat for several minutes before he smiled quizzically, arranged the papers neatly on his desk, and buzzed Denise. 'I'll have that coffee now,' he said brightly.

He was certainly safe now. He'd incinerated the bloodied shirt, and dropped the knife overboard, a kilometre out to sea.

Halcyon Days

There are usually times in every life when people look back over the struggle of the years to consider where they are now, and feel well satisfied. They might even do so with smugness, believing that they have earned the contentment they enjoy from their own efforts. Others give silent thanks, knowing that their comfortable lives have been decided by forces beyond them. And there'll always be those who won't ever feel this peace, either because life is unkind, or because they'll always find something to complain about.

Greg and Dana Bannerman were humble about their satisfaction with the way things had turned out for them. They lived in a comfortable house in a good suburb; the mortgage was manageable because both of them worked; they had Toby, a ten-year-old, who was happy at school and little trouble at home; and they both enjoyed their work as teachers, Greg as a high school teacher of English, and Dana as a fourth class teacher at the local primary school.

If they'd been asked whether or not they had a happy marriage, and one of Dana's friends did from time to time, they both would have answered with an unequivocal 'yes'. Of course there were differences, but they found these endearing rather than irritating. Comments like 'He has to be on time – hates being late', and 'She has absolutely no sense of direction', were always conferred light-heartedly.

'You should have seen him today,' he tells Dana enthusiastically. He's just returned home from collecting Toby from his weekend cricket. Toby too is excited and bright-eyed, and Dana stops chopping bacon at the kitchen bench, and prepares herself eagerly for the blow-by-blow.

'We won, Mum,' Toby can't wait. 'Thirty-four not out. My highest score. Mr Munroe said I can bat at number five from now on.'

'He was terrific,' Greg pats him on the shoulder, 'and that drive through mid-on to the boundary, that was really something.'

'That's wonderful,' Dana is all smiles. 'We're proud of you, Toby,' she adds, looking with equal fondness at the two men in her life. She'll ask him to set the table for their dinner guests later. To do so now might seem to be a penalty.

The Sedgmans and Tates are regular dinner guests. The Sedgmans are happy-go-lucky, fun to be with, and their very bulk seems to lend heft to their undiluted views on any topic. The Tates are more reserved, some say more refined, and both Greg and Dana sense something amiss in their relationship, some disturbing undercurrent. Paula Tate is the one who asks Dana about the happiness of her marriage. Dana is wary of doing the same.

The talk begins with questions about work, dominated by the men. Paula is a legal secretary, and Julie Sedgman doesn't work. Once the lamb rack arrives, and the wine is poured, the talk moves to issues.

'Do you teach the kids at school anything about domestic violence?' Paula asks.

Greg explains the relevant sections of the personal development curriculum dealing with respect for each other. The buffoon in Dale Sedgman suggests the need to keep women in their place, and is shushed by Julie. Colin Tate argues the issues, deploring any violence, particularly that against women.

'Amen,' says Dana.

Paula asked the question but has said nothing.

'That went well,' Dana says. 'They liked the lamb and mint sauce. A long day but a satisfying one.' She is standing naked beside the bed as Greg undresses. They lie down together.

'Aren't we lucky?' she continues, thinking of the day that has passed, and revisiting the dinner conversation. 'Do you think they're as happy as we are? I mean, what do you make of the Tates?'

'Probably not.' Greg evades further analysis. 'We are fortunate. These are certainly halcyon days.'

'What days?' Dana queries.

'Halcyon days. Halcyon is Greek for a kingfisher,' Greg explains. 'It lays its eggs and incubates in calm waters before the winter solstice. Halcyon days are times of peace and prosperity.'

'Well, here's to halcyon days,' and Dana raises a pretend glass.

*

'You've pushed too hard again,' Dana admonishes him when he returns from his early morning jog the next day. 'You look done in.'

He's standing on the porch, bent over, hands on his knees, and breathing hard, beneath a constipated sun that peers through rags of early morning cloud.

'Is everything all right?' she asks, suddenly concerned, and moving towards him. 'Do you need a glass of water?'

His eyes are adrenalin-wide, and there is a slight hint of foam around his mouth.

'Sit down,' she orders, leading him to the swinging seat.

'Two hooligans,' he begins, and needs to take a deep breath. 'Two hooligans were beating up a man. They saw me running towards them, but they didn't stop. One punched him in the face, knocked him down, and the other started kicking him when he was on the ground.'

Now that he's freed the words, they begin to flow, a haemorrhage of indignation.

'Late teens, early twenties, shaved heads, piercings, tattoos, really rough-looking. They smirked when I got nearer, as if they were daring me…and they didn't stop.' He pauses. A loaded pause. He craves her understanding, her comfort.

But she wants proof of his nobility, the need for faith in love that reaches out. 'What did you do?' she asks impatiently.

He replays it in his mind. The older victim, well-dressed for work with his shock of sandy brown hair, just like his own father, the surprise on his face, then a look of pained non-comprehension as if the act needed an intelligible explanation, the briefcase thrown into nearby bushes, and the victim on the ground muddied by early dew, twisting, shielding his face from the kicks.

'What did you do?' she asks.

Two young men dressed in dirty army fatigues, intent to hurt, and to humiliate. His stopping, or at least slowing to consider, to come up with an instant plan. Both men observing him, one from a scarred face, no doubt the legacy of previous assaults when he wasn't in control. And smirking. A look that was surely an invitation. Do you want some too, it seemed to say.

'What did you do?' she asks.

Yes, he was scared, his concern at such an outrage tempered by fear, a lack of breath, possibly from jogging, and a heaviness as if his body was flaccid and unable to move. But worst of all was the powerlessness, the indecision.

'You surely didn't let...' she asks again, and reads the answer in his face.

His importuning eyes confuse her allegiances. 'I probably saved his life,' Greg defends himself, aware of how hollow it sounds. 'They stopped soon after that.'

The lame bravado falls between them heavily to settle like a quilt.

How soon, she wants to ask, but doesn't.

'Greg, it was only last night we were all talking about this. How many times have you and I spoken about it...the need to rid the world of violence.' Her wearied feeling dies, and the clichés wither on her tongue. And as though he has been guilty of a great hypocrisy, 'You were always our great apologist!'

She quietly leaves the porch and retreats inside the house, making him feel like an accomplice in the act. The air is heavy with recrimination. He also feels annoyed. What did you want me to do, he feels like calling after her. Wade in boots and all? And what if they had a knife? A gun?'

Toby is at the breakfast table when he enters the house, and aware that something is not quite right, so there is no opportunity to continue the discussion.

'One thing's for sure,' he whispers to her, 'next time I see them, they'll get a thrashing they won't soon forget.'

In the cider light outside, the orb of sun retreats behind a cloud.

*

Dana refuses to admit that anything is wrong, but a shadow has been cast over the relationship. It is as if she has withdrawn into her shell, that some of her earlier *joie de vivre* has been scrubbed away.

She continues as she has before, but something is missing in how she behaves with Greg. She is attentive to him, and they continue to make love, or at least to go through the motions. At times she is animated, and some of her signature cheekiness returns, but it seems as though she is fighting her gloom, determined to stop it from taking over.

The change in Greg is even more marked, his depression more obvious. He becomes easily frustrated when students are refractory at school, when a task at home gets the better of him, or when his computer doesn't behave. He puts off the Sedgmans and Tates on more than one occasion.

After ten days, during which the incident has been ignored, he confronts Dana. 'Tell me, just tell me,' he nearly shouts, 'what do you think I should have done?'

Dana is so shocked by the outburst, she doesn't reply before Greg resumes.

'Would you have been happier if I'd come back with my front teeth missing, a few broken ribs, and a bunged-up eye, or,' and he becomes so aggressive that Dana begins to cry, 'perhaps a broken arm or spine? If it'd been Colin Tate, he'd still be running away.'

Worse is to come. They'd eaten late because of a school staff meeting that Dana had to attend, and when they'd finished the meal, she asks Toby if he would do the washing up, his rostered night to do so.

'When I've watched my show, Mum,' Toby answers.

Greg leaps from his seat, shouts, 'Don't you dare answer back,' and slaps Toby across the face.

The silence is palpable. Time is frozen. Seconds pass. Only faint canned laughter comes from the television in the family room, mocking the drama. Dana is horrified, and looks from Greg to Toby and back, her mouth open, before she moves to Toby and holds him. Greg's anger is gone as quickly as it arrived, and he too looks shocked as if he's only just realised the magnitude of what he's done.

To add to Greg's misery, Toby, his eyes filled with tears, turns to him, and says, 'Sorry, Dad,' before Dana whisks him away.

Greg sits in a heavy silence, never having felt so forlorn.

Later that night, he creeps into Toby's room to apologise. Toby is still shaken. He's never been struck before, but is relieved that his father is no longer hostile. And it is no half-hearted apology.

'What I did was unforgivable, Toby,' and he pauses. 'It won't happen again. How about a half-century on Saturday?' He tries to return things to a cheerful normality.

'Sure, Dad,' Toby replies without enthusiasm. 'Why don't you go and see that man in the hospital. The one who got hurt?'

Greg does, bowled over by his son's percipience. Dana must have explained why he'd been behaving differently.

The name makes it more real. Graham Wearing. Small-business owner. No longer a faceless victim. Identifiable flesh and bone, probably loved by a wife like he is, hopefully. Graham is grateful for his visit, and understanding when he explains his part in the drama. He tells of how he hurried over as the men were finishing beating him. He doesn't say he scared them away, and he doesn't say they took no notice of him. Graham wasn't even aware that someone else was there, and thanks Greg for his intervention.

Greg's talk with Graham makes a difference to his spirits.

For a week after the incident with Toby, things between Dana and Greg are strained. Dana knows that Greg is remorseful, but the sudden flaring of his temper disturbs her. Greg had spoken to her before he apologised to Toby, and his obvious distress softens her reaction. She holds him, but that image of the slap, and Toby's bewilderment and pain is frozen in time.

'Please, never...' and she doesn't finish. She doesn't have to.

Greg is attentive to them both in the weeks that follow. Toby does score a half century at cricket, and that, with Greg's praise, goes a long way to restoring the bond between them.

He hasn't been intimate with Dana, though he desperately wants to be. But she isn't dismissive or cold. She gently asks him to give her a little more time, and takes his hand as they lie in bed talking of the day's happenings.

And time does make a difference. Dana is able to overcome her feelings of withdrawal. She realises that Greg needs the support that he's never asked for or needed before, and with that knowledge her responsiveness returns.

One Saturday afternoon a month after the incident, when life seems to have returned to its halcyon days, Dana, paying for her goods at the supermarket, hears shouting from the car park where Greg is waiting for her, and recognises his voice. She hurries outside to see Greg berating a bellicose-looking man in his forties, and standing close to him in a threatening manner.

'Who the hell do you think you are?' the man snarls. 'It's none of your bloody business.'

The man's wife stands by his side, looking timid and very uncomfortable. 'Please go,' she says to Greg. 'Please.'

A small crowd is gathering, and Dana, not wanting her husband to make a scene where she shops at least twice a week, pulls him away. They drive off quickly.

Once home, Greg explains that the man had been belittling his wife, telling her she was useless, calling her names, and that he'd pushed her so that she bumped her side on the bonnet of their car. He'd intervened and, yes, he had threatened the man.

Dana isn't pleased. Greg may have intervened when a woman was being maltreated, but there are some situations it is better to ignore. The man may have been right in telling him it was none of his business. There were other more appropriate courses of action.

Her real concern is Greg's anger. Even in the telling, he is becoming agitated, and this persists throughout the night. He can't let it go.

Greg is sceptical of the psychologist they visit together at Dana's insistence. He is pleasant enough, sitting back in his leather studded chair, listening to Greg's account of witnessing the attack on Graham, speaking of the impact of stress and anxiety on the brain that can lead to the production of stress hormones and the possible loss of memory and ability to reason.

Greg becomes impatient when he speaks of the need to talk to friends and not isolate himself. He calls it 'a grounding exercise', the need 'to be validated'. It is the sort of common sense Greg tells his year eight students.

Dana and Greg do listen more attentively when he outlines a typical chain of feelings following an incident of this sort: assumptions like failing to cope, underlying feelings like powerlessness, negative perceptions of self like feeling inadequate, leading to negative perceptions of others, and finally anti-social behaviour. He seems particularly interested in Greg's guilt.

'Well, I'm not sure where that got us,' Greg remarks as they drive away.' But he doesn't want Dana to feel discouraged. 'He's probably right about the negative perceptions of myself and therefore others.'

Dana is interested in the focus of the psychologist on Greg's guilt.

*

Greg has continued to take his early morning run before breakfast. He isn't a believer in lightning striking twice in the same place, so he isn't fearful of going, and Graham's attackers have no reason to target him. He could probably outrun them anyway if they decide to give chase. He has often wondered what he would do if he does see them again.

He is feeling buoyant. The sky is already a pale blue, deepening in colour, and Sandy, the grinning Labrador from the corner house, runs beside him for several blocks, leaving him before he enters Boronia Park.

As he does so, he sees two young men eighty metres away pushing a third man backwards and forwards between them. They aren't the same men as before. One man slaps the victim's face and pushes him to the other, who stands a couple of metres away. This man does the same before pushing him back. Their voices are raised and the abused man, better dressed than his attackers, is pleading with them to stop.

The victim is thrown to the ground, but the two men don't kick him. They continue the verbal barrage and stand, grinding their boots on his hands and chest instead.

Only thirty metres away now, Greg can see the muddy boot imprints on the man's shirt, and the torn away buttons.

For an instant, the early images return, the smirking 'do you want some too' look, the brutality of the kicking, the look of non-comprehension on Graham's face. And the same indecision returns, the same leaden feeling, the same fear. But only for an instant.

Greg has covered the last thirty metres in a couple of seconds. The men have stopped but are not chastened.

'Bugger off,' one says.

'Get lost,' from the other. 'It's nothing to do with you.'

Greg doesn't move. And they make no move towards him.

'I'll go,' he says, recalling later that he must have sounded ridiculously urbane, 'when this man,' and he points to the man on the ground, 'comes with me.'

'Do you want your face punched in?' the more aggressive of the two men snarls, moving towards him.

'If that's what it takes,' Greg replies, raising his hands, battling to keep his nerve, for the first time knowing that he will not walk away. Not this time. And he readies himself for the attack, realising that a beating is the likely outcome.

'I must have looked menacing,' he tells Dana later. 'They probably thought I could do some real damage,' and feeling exalted, 'I reckon I could have.'

'Come on, Kurt,' the less aggressive man says. 'We've had our fun,' and while the first man seems reluctant to do so, waving his fist threateningly at Greg, they swagger away.

Greg helps the man on the ground to rise, and is thanked profusely. The man swears that he isn't hurt, except for a bruised ego, and shaking Greg's hand, asking if there is anything he can do in return, walks gingerly towards the town.

Dana can't believe the change in Greg, not then when he returns home in high spirits, greeting Toby with a high five, and hugging her as she ladles out the porridge, and not afterwards when a load seems to have been lifted from his shoulders, and he behaves like his normal self.

'A century next weekend,' he says to Toby when his son leaves for school.

'Tonight, Josephine,' he winks at Dana when his son has gone. 'Perhaps it's about time we had the Sedgmans and Tates for dinner.'

He leaves for school whistling, doing a little comical skip in his gait for Dana's benefit as he walks to the car.

*

Greg doesn't know that Dana, after months of searching, has found the original edition of *Bleak House*, the Dickens novel he'd been searching for and unable to find. It was in an old second-hand bookshop, and she's had the book gift-wrapped to present to him that very night.

He doesn't know that when she had been to the city the weekend before to meet old school friends, she had also gone to the exclusive lingerie shop, and purchased some very sexy black silk lingerie with pink ribbons that she plans to slip into after the special meal of beef bourguinon she'd prepare for that night when she arrives home from her teaching duties. She'll brush out her hair and let it fall below her shoulders. Stand before him.

And he certainly doesn't know of her meeting to thank three men, three colleagues from her school, and how they laughed, recounting and ribbing each other about their acting performances in Boronia Park that morning.

Mad Susan: A Love Story

Sometimes the inexplicable happenings to people can only be accounted for by the paranormal or supernatural. Some people dismiss these experiences as fate, a vague notion of something that was meant to be, something governed by mysterious forces. Others give credit to a more omniscient power. And of course there'll always be those who'll simply say it was a matter of the odds.

Jo and I gave credit to an omniscient power for our reconciliation. We'd gone our separate ways after a bitter argument. Ego and self-righteousness made each of us implacable, and questioning whatever it was that attracted us to each other in the first place. We were miserable, but neither of us was prepared to concede. It was the intervention of a complete stranger that made us realise our argument had been groundless, and that neither of us was more to blame than the other. It had been a valuable and humbling lesson.

All had been restored between us for a fortnight when we visited Lake Parramatta for the first time, a picturesque place where a deep olive-green lake is surrounded by tall gums, many of them clawing their footing into a rocky foreshore, and where there are large grassy expanses with picnic tables, pergolas and a small kiosk.

We usually began our outings with morning tea. Jo could not function, or so she said, without her morning coffee, so we went to the kiosk, made our way to a small table in the corner, but were diverted to another by the waiter.

'So has he been today?' an odd-looking woman wheeling her tiny luggage to the same corner table asked as soon as we had been escorted from it.

The waiter shook his head. 'Not today, Susan. Perhaps tomorrow,' he said.

'Mad Susan's table,' he whispered as he came for our order with a literalness-cum-sobriquet, and a hint of apology. 'And by the way, she doesn't mind being called that.'

Mad Susan didn't order. From what the waiter had said, we assumed that she was a regular, and that her order was always the same. She was a woman of indeterminate years, but from a heavily wrinkled face and slight stoop, we reckoned she was in her sixties or early seventies. She had greying hair that must have been raven in earlier years, and she wore a shapeless floral skirt, a white blouse, floppy hat and track shoes. She had a kindly face, but one that seemed to be set with an inquisitive look as if life was a constant surprise. She sat staring across the lake, waiting for her regulation order. An assortment of coins was neatly piled on the table.

We didn't pay her much attention as we drank our coffee, chatted and left. There was a scenic forty-minute walk around the lake through native bush and across small creeks made passable with stepping stones. When we returned from the walk, we saw Mad Susan sitting near the lake's edge below the path, looking across the sunlit olive of the lake, watching the ducks in gleaming phalanx and the sulphur-crested cockatoos playing tag between the towering gums.

She rose quickly to her feet as she saw us approach along the path. 'I wonder,' she said, 'if you've seen a man, about so high?' and she motioned with a benedictory hand. 'Grey eyes and very regal, possibly in khaki slacks and a mustard top.'

'No, sorry,' I said.

'We've been on the walk,' Jo added. 'We didn't pass anyone of that description.'

Mad Susan returned to her spot with no apparent sign of disappointment while we sat nearby, enjoying the foreshore's wattle mirroring gold across the lake, and observing her accosting every passer by with the same enquiry.

'Have you possibly seen a man, grey eyes? He might be wearing khaki slacks and a mustard top.'

Indulgent smiles invited the description they were loath to hear before they'd shake their heads. No one enquired further. A few said 'sorry' as if apology was warranted.

We returned to the kiosk for lunch, and when the waiter took our order, I asked after Mad Susan. Heads from a number of nearby tables turned my way, people who had obviously been approached as we had.

The elderly proprietor came out from behind the counter to explain. 'She hasn't missed a day in well over thirty years,' he said. 'And always here, the same old floppy hat, the umbrella all skew-whiff with broken spokes, and wheeling her little odds and ends.' He paused. He had a captive audience. 'I guess some feelings can't be numbed by time. To keep believing blunts the loneliness.'

The people at some of the nearby tables looked across to Jo and me and either shrugged or smiled as the proprietor returned to his place behind the counter.

'Tomorrow,' Mad Susan called cheerily to the proprietor with a scratchy voice as we finished our lunch.

All eyes turned to watch her shambling gait as she left, and time stood still until the squeaking wheels were heard no more, and silence for a moment overwhelmed.

*

Several days after our visit to Lake Parramatta, we were returning in the car from lunching with Jo's parents.

'I've been thinking a lot about that woman, Mad Susan,' Jo said, 'and I was wondering if there was anything we could…' She saw me smile, and hesitated. Then she smiled too. 'I should have known,' she continued, 'that you'd be thinking the same thing. Great minds. But is there really anything we could do?'

'Probably not,' I answered. 'We have nothing to go on at all, and I don't think she'll be a lot of help.'

'No,' Jo said resignedly. 'But fate was kind to us. Remember that complete stranger? It all came out of the blue. Obviously it was meant to be. Perhaps we can play the role of complete stranger for Mad Susan.'

So it was that we returned to the lake with a mission.

Jo was more optimistic than me, believing it only right that fate smile on our efforts. 'That poor woman,' she kept saying. 'I'm quite sure it's going to turn out really well.'

We found Mad Susan sitting by the foreshore where she'd accosted us before.

'Could you tell me,' she said approaching, and obviously not remembering us, 'if you've seen a man, about so tall, grey eyes, very distinguished-looking, khaki trousers, mustard top?'

I allowed Jo to take the lead. 'Can you tell me his name?' she said gently.

'You've seen him!' Mad Susan was suddenly alert.

'No, no.' Jo was quick and careful not to raise her hopes. 'It might help a little if people,' and she distanced us from a specific interest, 'had a little more information to go on…a name, a more detailed description…'

Mad Susan was very willing to share all she knew, and happy that someone was giving her more than a cursory interest, but her memory was clouded and she was not very articulate. She only knew his first name. Alan. They'd not swapped surnames, and had only met once, but what a meeting it was, she told us with gleaming eyes. Her description didn't go far beyond what she'd related to passers-by.

Jo was downcast. I was disappointed, but my expectations weren't as high. We weren't detectives, but if we'd had a surname, that would have been a starting point. There would surely have been government departments, social welfare, professional associations, even charities that might have records. How do you find someone with only the name Alan, who could be anywhere in the country, or in the world, and who mightn't look anything like a sketchy thirty-year-old description. He mightn't even be alive. But Jo was determined not to give up.

The plan we agreed on was to assume that Alan was a local, and that someone in the area might know of him. It was a long shot, because he could have come from anywhere, but we decided to ask the local shopkeepers and businesses, and people in nearby homes. We wouldn't door-knock, but we'd stop to enquire of anyone we saw in a front yard.

We devoted two full days to this. Jo enquired at the local shops. I approached local businesses and investigated other organisations. People were keen to help and took an interest, but while it was an established area around the lake, the great majority of shops and businesses were under more recent ownership. Very few could boast thirty years with the same staff. We spoke to a few home-dwellers, some of whom had been at the same address for over thirty years, but were met with shakes of the head, except for the few who saw it as an opportunity to reminisce:

'There was Alan Pettit, he and I played rugby together for years, had a lovely wife…now what was her name, Lydia, that's it, but he wasn't tall, only about five four, built like a tank, though. Long dead now.'

'We tried, that's the important thing,' I told a disconsolate Jo. 'It was a tall order. All we had was a first name, and for all we know, that wasn't his real name anyway.'

When we returned to the lake one afternoon a few days later, and after Mad Susan had gone home, we were approached in the kiosk by a well-dressed man in his late forties.

'Are you the couple asking about a tallish grey-eyed gent called Alan?' he asked. 'Here about thirty years back?'

Jo could hardly contain her excitement.

'My father was mates with an Alan. He lived a few streets away. Tall. I met him a few times when I was a lad and he came to the house.

Not sure about his eyes. They might well have been grey. Left the area suddenly after some personal tragedy, but my father knows where he is. Anyway, it's probably nothing but I thought I'd tell you next time I came.'

Jo was delighted. 'Fate has certainly been kind,' she enthused, and gave me a celebratory kiss.

*

We learned from the man's father that Alan Blessing had moved to a small house in a neighbouring suburb when the family had dwindled in size, and were warned that he was feeling the impact of the passing years.

'We'll just march up to the door,' Jo said excitedly. 'I'll take him some of my famous pumpkin scones.'

'We need to be a bit careful,' I warned her. 'He might have no recollection of Mad Susan, or he might not even be proud of having met her, not if it was a betrayal of sorts.'

We saw him sitting in a rocker on the porch of an old fibro house with a pocket-handkerchief-sized front yard. We remained in the car across the street, collecting our thoughts, hearing his resonant 'g'days' as people passed. It was obvious he was well-known in the neighbourhood.

Jo and I both understood that we were thinking and feeling the same as each other again, contemplating the heft of life beyond his years, inventing fictional scenarios of what might have gone before, the fanciful imaginings of intimate realities. Perhaps one of those more meaningful realities involved Mad Susan.

What had been meant by the warning that Alan was 'feeling the impact of the passing years'? Was the endless succession of days in the hot porch sun melting his memories, congealing them like honey glaze and trapping thought?

He seemed glad when we introduced ourselves, saying that we were friends of his old mate, and was anxious to talk. He wasn't surprised by our visit, and didn't consider that it had any other purpose beyond the pleasure of sharing his company.

He spoke adoringly of his wife, interspersing his account with poetry he must have written years earlier to glorify her, and sometimes pausing for half a minute to savour his recollection. We thought it best to let him continue. We learnt that she was once pale and lissom, his word, and how the moonlight licked greedily on her bedroom nakedness, his image. And of how her voice was like running water as she called him a naughty boy. We'd learn in a few minutes that the memories of her final years were mercifully lost.

We were about to ask him the question we'd come for, when there was a 'yoo hoo' from next door, and a middle-aged woman, a Mrs Murton, entered from a gate in the fence. She was carrying a glad-wrapped plate, probably his dinner.

She led us aside to tell of her caring for Alan, as much as she was able to with her own family to care for. And she told us of his only son, the apple of his mother's eye, the grimy spectres in a trench, their camaraderie and mirth, the moment's folly as he stands, a sniper's bullet, and a life snuffed out. It was Alan's language she was repeating. She'd probably heard the story a dozen times.

We never did ask Alan the question. We both knew it wasn't 'our' Alan. It's hard to say how we knew, but we both thought the same. There were some things that didn't add up. He was ninety, so Mrs Murton told us, much older than Mad Susan. He was devoted to his family. And his eyes were a startling blue, not having changed with the blanching years. But much knowledge is intuitive. It wasn't him.

He thanked us when we departed, urging us to come again. We left him guiltily to the scones and the days that must have been far too long, and the nights that must have been longer still.

*

Once enquiries are made, and the word gets around, well-meaning people are keen to share their information. We received several calls on the phone, having left our numbers with the kiosk proprietor. Even though we only had sketchy information at best, it was clear that none of the prospects was the Alan we were looking for. Two calls were from women whose husbands had decamped with younger women.

We had virtually given up, when a call came from a woman whose husband was in a nearby nursing home. One of the occupants she told us was an Alan Lodge, late sixties, tall and with grey eyes. She knew nothing more of his history. We had decided to let go of what had become an obsession, but agreed to make this our last effort.

I was gratified that the nursing home was happy to let people, appropriately 'vetted', take the residents out for brief excursions. They were well pleased when I nominated Alan Lodge, referring to him as a friend of a friend. Jo and I agreed that I would take him for morning tea to a nearby café while she remained at the nursing home and tried to find out what she could about Alan's past.

His room was one of many off a stone-coloured linoleum corridor. It had a single bed, a wardrobe and a small writing desk. Two tasteless mass-produced abstract prints hung on the walls. It was sombre, though sunlight was trying to squeeze through shuttered slats. A porcelain vase of orange gerberas was wilting on the sill.

Our first reaction was positive. He was tall, the right age, and his eyes were grey. He wasn't overjoyed to see us, and seemed apprehensive, but we'd been well briefed and warned not to expect too much. We'd both later imagine him swaddled in his bed, his only immunity from anxiety, and his only comfort in the things he knows: the elaborate cornices and frosted ceiling light, the door that opens on his wandering thoughts to capture muted voices from adjacent rooms, the pills and prophylactic words at eight a.m.

We did our best to make him feel comfortable. Jo even brought her signature pumpkin scones, but they didn't excite much interest.

I made sure that he was presentable, found an old maroon cardigan in his wardrobe and, leaving Jo sitting on his bed, we took our leave, saying our goodbyes to the nursing staff. He followed at a snail's pace, though I didn't take his arm. It was important that he feel independent.

The day was picture book. Blue sky. Warm. No wind. But the storm was his. We'd only gone a few hundred metres, halfway to the café, when the clouds were louring for him, catching him in indecision's parody. He'd move a step forward, look anxiously around, then take another step backwards, looking stricken, before he turned and, taking no heed of me, headed home in a hurry. I had no option but to follow. Why force challenges he dare not face?

'Alan,' the sister held my look and shrugged. 'Are you sure, Alan? It's such a lovely day.'

And so the special morning I'd planned with what I'd hoped would be a pleasant morning tea, and an opportunity for him to talk, became gin rummy with the three of us in the room that was shrinking with him, and with stewed tea and ginger snaps. He was silent for most of the time, often watching us both with curiosity and concern as if he'd just seen us for the first time, yet he showed a flicker of pleasure when he won at cards.

After an hour with Alan, Jo signalled that it was time to go, from which I inferred that she had discovered something.

'Would you like us to come again?' I felt I had to ask.

He looked vacant and said nothing, and I knew he'd listen to our departing steps, tick tock receding along the linoleum corridor to fade into a welcome silence.

'I found a letter,' Jo said, 'in a wardrobe drawer,' and as we climbed into the car, she took it from her handbag and unfolded it.

'Jo,' I protested, 'it's not yours to take.'

'I know,' she replied. 'It's not right. I think he's beyond reading it now, though. Perhaps we can take it back later some time. But I knew you'd want to read it, and know the exact wording of it. Alan wrote it, but he never posted it.'

I took the letter from Jo and read it aloud as we sat in the front seat of the car.

My dear Susan,

I hope you don't mind me using the possessive 'my', and after having only met once. Yesterday was the most wonderful, and at the same time the most terrible day of my life.

It was the most wonderful because I met you. I have recalled every word we spoke, every one of the looks I read on your face. Have you ever felt so completely absorbed in someone, that nothing else seems real, as if the rest of the world is tapping on the window pane of your being trying to get in, and can't. I hadn't.

Remember I said that my divorce was to be finalised in a couple of weeks. Well, when I arrived home from seeing you, my wife reported that she had a particularly aggressive cancer. True, because she showed me the medical report.

I know I said we'd meet tomorrow (same place, same time) but I hope you'll understand if I can't be there. She's not handling it at all well! Things may be very unsettled for a while, and I have to give my support.

You know you're where my heart is. Is it silly to say I'm missing you when less than a day has passed? I'll try to get someone to take this letter to the man at the kiosk to pass on to you.

Love, Alan.

(Twenty-nine days later.) She's gone. It was not a pleasant end. I feel drained. I also feel guilty – her having to confront her marriage break-up in her dying days. I think I could have done more. I know I could have. Lots for me to do now.

You may think that I haven't had the time to think of you. Please don't. I shut out everything else but you when I go to bed at night. Such a relief and pleasure.

Sorry I haven't sent this letter yet. You must be wondering about me.

(Forty-seven days later.) Haven't sent these ramblings yet. Sorry. I feel very down. A real mix of warring emotions.

Do you still care, Susan? Did that day at the lake really happen? Or am I imagining it, reading too much into it? Was it a fleeting need in a passing moment in each of our lives that propelled us together?

'Well, it's certainly our Alan,' I said, refolding the letter. 'I wonder what happened after that,' and we drove home in silence.

*

We sat in the kiosk having our morning tea. It was another luminous day of sun-drenched blue. A flock of sulphur-crested cockatoos flew from tree to tree screeching. We could see Mad Susan sitting some eighty metres away in the second spot she'd claimed as her own by the foreshore.

A couple passed, and she rose to her feet. She raised her hand, no doubt demonstrating the height of a man in khaki slacks and mustard top.

We'd come to tell her what we'd found, but we both felt uneasy about it.

'We've come this far,' Jo said. 'I suppose we owe it to her, but something is warning me against telling her.'

'I don't know,' I answered. 'We've said a lot about the part fate plays. It's been kind to us before. It was kind again this time. But if we don't tell her, aren't we just playing God?'

Jo considered this for half a minute while I too sat thinking. I felt the same concern as Jo.

'We could give her the letter.' Jo was anxious for a satisfying conclusion.

'Not sure about the letter,' I said. 'Do you think it might be disturbing for her? But I think we agree that Alan's whereabouts should remain a secret. Better she preserve a meaningful fantasy than indulge a suspect reality.'

We were so lost in our own thoughts that we didn't hear Mad Susan approach.

'Bye,' she called cheerily. 'Tomorrow then.'

All eyes turned to watch her retreat as the sound of squeaking wheels faded to silence.

The Kiss

'You know why you're here, Tom. There has to be some explanation for this. Some sort of misunderstanding perhaps?'

Tom gave a resigned shrug. Better to learn the limits of his offence, if that's what it was. How it had been constructed and reconstructed. What another's memory had done with the creep of feeling from each imagined revisiting. There'd been a complaint, but was it reported as some petty and forgiveable lapse, a grievance that could be dismissed with a smiling 'There, that's been dealt with', or was it to be hauled from a misguided innocence to a serious personal affront. To be waved with the banner of persecution. Proclaimed as an example of the dragon-slayer seeking justice from the oppressor.

'Well, is it true, Tom? She said you kissed her.'

'Yes, I suppose I did.'

'You suppose. Surely you either did or didn't. I'll take that as a yes.'

Tom remained silent, head down, already looking beaten. Or was it possibly growing guilt or contrition? Whatever, it halted the dean's emerging irritation. She was a few years younger than Tom, with cropped, mousy-coloured hair, and power-dressed for eagerly anticipated promotion. But they'd always enjoyed a good professional relationship.

'You'd better tell me what happened, Tom,' she said more gently.

At least he was still Tom. Not stripped of identity, to suffer the anonymity of the miscreant. That, Tom reckoned, showed some confederacy.

'I don't know what to say,' he said quietly, deep in thought. 'I kissed her. We'd been discussing the assignment. She hadn't understood what was being asked. It was the one on reinforcement. She was battling to understand that negative reinforcement…'

'Tom, I don't need to know what your assignment was.' There was no impatience in her interruption. 'Just tell me what happened.'

'I don't remember how it all changed. It was reinforcement one minute, and her marriage the next. At first she was curious, bright even. Then she was sombre.'

He paused, recalling how forlorn she had looked, sitting cross-legged in her ragged denim jeans, urgency in her eyes, her long, dark hair gathered to the front over one shoulder, watching him intently as she spoke.

'For a long while, she'd suspected there was something between her husband and his secretary. She was always mentioned in their conversations, he danced with her a bit too intimately at the office party, she found notes and receipts for gifts, smears on his shirts that might have been face powder, rouge, that sort of thing. Then work demands increased, when they never had before, and he had to stay back. Would come home late, seemed to have lost interest in her. She said something, rather delicately, but enough to lead me to believe that sex between them rarely happened, and when it did, it was far from tender, even rough, a frustrated longing that she wasn't able to satisfy, or a punishment.'

'And that's when you kissed her.' The dean leant forward, a gesture of sorts, like meeting him halfway, reading the resignation in his lowered eyes.

He nodded. How much more did the dean need to know? The why of it all hardly mattered. Judgements were based on actions. And how could he articulate the why anyway? It was an impulse, a rare moment of connection, a gesture of tenderness and empathy. He'd leant forward as she'd looked up, and the kiss lightly brushed her lips. She'd looked startled, but only for a moment. At the time, he thought she seemed pleased. Or at least more at ease. After all, she'd revealed the most intimate details of her life. His kiss was a statement, however clumsy, that he was in tune with her feelings. If only he'd known it would be so unwelcome.

How do you dissect a kiss? Surely they're not all the same. This was a kiss that came from feeling, gentle and sweet, a fleeting touch that leaves a taste of tenderness. It wasn't the more vigorous kiss where couples search for meaning or try to find themselves in each other's mouths. And it certainly wasn't the kiss offered in lust. God forbid that he might be tarred with the brush of the abuser.

'I get it, Tom,' the dean commented after a lengthy silence. 'That puts me in the picture. I'm really sorry about this,' and she reached out as though she were going to place a consoling hand on his shoulder, but thought better of it, and left her hand in the air, making it a gesture.

'The thought that you were trying to, you know…' she half-smiled, 'is ridiculous. You'd have to agree, though, in retrospect,' she felt the need to counsel, and to state what officialdom decreed, 'it was foolish. You can never be certain how something like that is seen by others. A man of – what is it, fifty-four, fifty five? – kissing a much younger female student, is not a good look, however innocent or caring the motive, particularly in this day and age.'

Tom watched the dean. Watched her lips moving, even saw the concern in her eyes. For half a minute he didn't hear the words. He felt he was dissociated, looking on at someone else's unfolding scenario. Not grasping how the situation applied to him. Am I remorseful, he asked himself. What am I really feeling?

'You'll have to apologise,' he suddenly heard the dean say, leaving no doubt as to his culpability. 'Something low-key,' she said, feeling sorry for him, leaving him to wonder what a low-key apology involved. 'I'm sure it will all go away with a minimum of fuss.'

*

'I kissed a girl today. One of the students,' he told his wife of thirty years.

'Oh yes,' Beth answered light-heartedly, undisturbed as she added pasta to the boiling water, but seeing that Tom was looking uncomfortable, she left the saucepan to boil, rubbed her hands on her apron, and sat down beside him on the divan in the family room next to the kitchen.

'And what sort of kiss was it?' she quipped, trying to lighten his mood. 'Was it like this?' and she gently pecked him on the cheek, her eyes alight with mischief. 'Or was it like this?' She pulled him down on the lounge and gave him a prolonged kiss on the mouth. 'I'll bet it wasn't like that,' she said playfully.

He could taste the pasta sauce she had tested for flavour and spooned into another saucepan.

'The student complained. Went to the dean. I was called to account.'

'They're not serious,' Beth protested, and could see Tom's uneasiness. 'You'd better tell me exactly what happened.' She was no longer playful.

Tom told her, his explanation fuller than the one he gave the dean. It was more an account of how he'd felt as the talk with the student unfolded. Beth had been privy to his innermost feelings for half a lifetime, and understood him when they both knew others wouldn't.

'So what happens now?' she asked, her concern transparent on a face pink and damp from her cooking.

'I've received a reprimand, and I have to apologise to the student.' He held up a hand to halt Beth's protest. 'I don't blame Shirley. I think she was sympathetic, but she has to follow official procedure.'

'Pasta bolognese, yum!' Cassie, their teenage daughter, entered in a rush, dropping her school bag on the tiled kitchen floor and bringing their talk to an abrupt end. 'My favourite.'

'Enter the whirlwind,' Beth said laughingly, suddenly brightening. 'You must have been able to smell it from, well, from wherever you've been.'

'Mum's pasta bol. I could smell it anywhere. And why is Daddy so quiet? Did I interrupt something?'

She approached him from behind, and threw her arms around his neck as he sat on the divan. At fifteen, Cassie was green-eyed, willowy and attractive. Nascent womanhood had been kind to her, opening a world of enticing possibilities that presently outweighed the other pitfalls of adolescence.

'Hard day at the office,' he answered jokingly, forcing good humour.

Beth and Cassie managed to keep up a continuous dialogue throughout the meal, while Tom tried his best to be his usual amiable self. Beth cast occasional concerned looks in his direction.

'You're in an unusually good mood,' he told Cassie. 'No doubt it has something to do with Leo,' and he winked at Beth across the table.

'Aw, Dad, that was ages ago,' Cassie said animatedly. 'It's Nicholas now.'

'Nicholas and not Leo?' Even Beth seemed surprised. 'And it wasn't ages ago with Leo. It was last week. I suppose it's a case of easy come, easy go. What happened to poor Leo?'

Cassie warmed to the chance of revealing her budding love life, proud of her recently acquired sex appeal.

'He's a real sleaze, Mum. He tried to put his tongue in my mouth. Yuk.'

'Cassie!' Beth remonstrated.

Cassie laughed, pleased by her worldliness. 'Don't tell me you never did that with Dad.'

Beth looked across the table at Tom and shrugged.

Tom smiled lamely, and ate in silence as the two women of the household chatted.

*

He'd thought about the apology for some time with a mixture of feelings. A bald 'I'm sorry' and a sudden retreat would not be sufficient, for her or for him. He needed to explain. He needed her to see the reason, to understand that his action was the result of caring. And he had to dispel the idea that he was a predator who took advantage of the vulnerable. If only she knew he'd been a great apologist for women confronting abuse.

She came reluctantly to a vacant staff common room. The dean had arranged it. She was dressed more formally than the usual student garb of torn and faded jeans and T-shirt. A tasteful navy blouse and beige skirt instead. She even wore a little make-up. Half-heels. Tom regarded it as a statement. The formality of apology demanded propriety.

The room had a kitchenette with sink, electric jug and microwave, deep green, slightly worn carpet, and two rows of facing lounge chairs in studded brown leather. Appropriate for affairs of state, if not affairs of the heart.

She sat opposite him, perching on the edge, rather than leaning back in the chair, knees together, ladylike, expectant.

'I thought we had a real rapport,' he began, hoping for eye contact. He didn't get it.

She seemed to give a half-nod, but looked uncomfortable, and sat with both hands clenched in her lap.

'You told me all about your marriage. Really personal things.'

He baulked at saying 'you remember'. That sounded too much like interrogation. He wanted to establish why he had reached out to her the way he had, a preamble to confessing to his overreaching. He tried to massage the thaw by recounting the personal nature of their conversation, and even revealing similar experiences in his own life. It didn't happen. Better to be more direct.

'I kissed you because I felt moved by your situation. It was because I cared, Nerida. I felt really sorry for you.'

He sensed her tighten. Realised the talk of his sympathy for her was a mistake. To be pitied was anathema. To act the way he had out of pity was probably worse.

'I'm not a sleaze, Nerida,' he whispered, feeling the heat at once behind his eyes. 'I detest men like that. Anyway, I'm sorry, really sorry if I upset you. At the time, it felt like a natural thing to do, but it may have been foolish.'

Nerida cocked her head at the 'may have been', but quickly recovered, resuming her blank stare.

There was an awkward silence before he asked her if she had anything to say.

It was a long time before she spoke. 'I accept your apology,' she said rather too formally, and not looking at him. Nothing more. She stood and turned to leave, uncertain of the departing courtesies for such an occasion. For a moment, turned towards him, she hesitated, about to speak, but the words didn't come, and she hurried away self-consciously.

Tom sat quietly. It was uncertain for how long. He was relieved and disappointed. It was over and done with. Apology accepted. That was a relief. Still, he'd hoped for some shared analysis of the dynamics, and for her to have a deeper appreciation of why he'd acted as he did. She might have shed more light on the impact it had on her, and why she saw fit to make a formal complaint rather than come to him. Was he that much of an ogre?

When several staff members entered for morning tea, calling out their hellos, and conferring loudly about their early classes, Tom thought they seemed more raucous than usual. He found their good cheer a challenge. He wasn't noticed leaving.

*

Catching the eight-seventeen bus to the university where he was employed as a teacher educator was a ritual. Why take a car when parking costs were so exorbitant, and the bus stopped at the gates? Apart from those making an occasional trip, many of the passengers had come to know each other: Bill, a gently spoken senior who visited the hospital every day to see his chronically ill wife; Mrs Luscombe, older still with silver-blue hair (she didn't like being called Beryl); Margaret, an attractive thirty-year-old mother who worked as a secretary; and several university students who were familiar by sight but not by name.

The day after his talk with the dean was bleak. The sky was a louring dark, and the bus was late, but just in time for him to escape the mist of rain. Not a good omen for those like Tom who thought the weather might have emotional portent.

'More last night on this Craig McCullough thing,' Margaret ventured after initial hellos. 'I'm so disappointed. Such a lovely man in *Dr Dale*. I liked him. I feel really let down. Do you think it's true?' she asked no one in particular.

The television news had presented a catalogue of complaints about McCullough's alleged sexual innuendo, his exposing himself to a woman, and his very inappropriate touching, often during performances of *Jesus Christ Superstar*. Pictures of three female actors were portrayed as victims, one obviously distressed as she recounted her experience. McCullough was seen protesting his innocence.

'Well, of course it's true,' Beryl responded through the pursed lips of conviction and rectitude. 'Surely you don't believe what you see them playing on television.' She was obviously on a favourite hobbyhorse, and one that excused her belittling of any challenger. 'They should all be castrated.'

'Who's they?' two of the university students chorused.

'Do you mean every male actor, or all men in general?' one of them continued, lightly mocking, intent to prick the inflated balloon of Beryl's bigotry. 'Castration's a bit severe, isn't it? I mean, cut off his balls? He didn't rape anyone.'

Beryl was annoyed, offended by the crudity, and interrupted in mid-flight. She was rarely challenged. 'They're all the same,' she mumbled.

'Thanks a lot,' one of the male students said softly, smiling at his friend, and winking at Tom.

'Well, that's my opinion,' Beryl said after a short silence, as if that were sufficient defence, and buried her head in a dog-eared paperback with obvious ill humour.

Margaret smiled at Tom and shrugged. He nodded and turned to look out the window at the thickening grey.

*

Tom began to catch a later bus in the mornings, and came home earlier when classes and meetings didn't demand his presence. His teaching was still sound but lacked his reputed energy. The students noticed his lack of animation, and chatted about it among themselves.

He abandoned working on the submission for a research grant for which he had recruited a team of colleagues.

He was pleasant at work but less gregarious, and seemed to spend more time closeted in his office, and away from the staff common room. He even stopped paying his two dollars for the weekly football tipping competition.

'You haven't been the same since, well, since our last talk a fortnight ago,' the dean, drawing him aside, commented. 'Is everything all right?'

'Yes, no problems,' Tom answered, forcing a weak smile.

'It's not!' The dean of course understood why. Tom was a respected and popular member of the faculty, and she felt she knew him well enough to contradict, even to challenge. 'It's not anything to do with that unfortunate incident with the student, is it?' she asked, knowing that it was. 'That's long forgotten. I'm quite sure she didn't blab about it, and none of the staff know.'

'I've been thinking about retirement,' Tom replied, skirting the dean's question.

'But why?' the dean asked, shocked.

'There comes a time, I suppose, in every life...well, you've no doubt heard all this many times before.'

The dean was caught off guard, and concerned, both for Tom and the faculty. 'We need to talk about this further, Tom,' she said. 'Don't be too hasty. How does next Thursday suit at two-thirty?'

Tom's lack of *joie de vivre* was even more apparent at home. He still asked Beth about her day, but seemed to be less engaged in listening. His usual ribbing of Cassie at the dinner table was replaced with polite enquiries.

One afternoon, Cassie returned home from school, barely able to contain her delight, having won a prestigious award for citizenship sponsored by the local Rotary Club. The award had been presented at a full school assembly by the local government member. Tom was proud, but embraced her tentatively, withdrawing quickly. She was hurt, and asked Beth if Dad was angry with her. They'd always been so demonstrative.

He abandoned some of the evening television shows he watched with Beth and Cassie, reality shows he lampooned as they shushed him, an after-dinner routine they all enjoyed, observed for the sake of family togetherness. Instead, he retreated to his study.

Beth was careful to choose the right moment to once again ask the inevitable question.

'I don't know what it is,' he told her that night as they undressed for bed, feeling miserable.

She felt that was barely a half-truth, yet she understood. She knew that sometimes the emotional impact of something trivial, a word or action, spreads through a person's being like a cancer.

'I did kiss her. Technically that's assault. Assault,' he repeated the word slowly, mulling over its implications. 'I didn't mean any harm by it,' he said miserably.

Beth knew when to listen, and when to interject. They sat together on the edge of the bed. This was a time to listen.

'As I get older, more things become problematic. The clear-cut things we argued so passionately for in our youth don't seem to be so clear-cut any more.' Despite his sombre mood, he suddenly thought of Beryl Luscombe, and had to smile, but it didn't disprove his point. There were few certainties, and the most passionate arguments were sometimes a disguise for serious doubts.

Beth looked at him curiously, and waited.

'What isn't clear-cut...' she eventually asked. 'Are you referring to the business with that girl?'

'I wonder,' he replied, his thoughts racing ahead, 'if, when we get older, emotion and thought become even more...' he struggled for a word, 'cloudy. Do the boundaries lose definition, do the feelings become more diffuse, do the blacks and whites become grey...do they merge?'

'I'm not sure I understand the significance of merging emotion,' Beth queried after another long silence. 'What emotions do you mean?'

'I'm sure we shed our inhibitions, but do we also lose our moral compass?' Tom answered, patting her thigh and taking her hand. 'I wonder,' he repeated, and left the sentence unfinished, absorbed in his thoughts.

As they both sat together silently on the side of the bed, facing the window, Beth put her arm around his shoulders, tousling his hair. She liked to mother him. The stars outside bathed the sky in a feast of milky light. A car turned into a gravel driveway next door. The engine stopped, a door slammed, and Cassie could be heard laughing at something on the television downstairs.

'My poor silly boy,' she said, drawing the curtains to join him in bed.

*

He sat in his office watching the swaying gum trees drop pale-bellied leaves in the autumn blue, aware of the paradox that everything remains the same but won't stand still. He felt strangely removed from the rows of shelved books, books that had engaged him lovingly over the years.

In half an hour, he would meet the dean. What would he say? He would be asked about retirement, probably cautioned against it. He would be told he still had a significant contribution to make. The dean obviously knew what bothered him. Or a small part of it anyway. She would try to reassure him, convince him of his popularity with students and staff, encourage him to confront his demons.

He could tell the dean that a few days after the incident with the girl, he'd garaged his car after returning from driving Cassie to a party, and contemplated the oak beam across the ceiling, wondering if it would support his weight. Of course he never would! They were idle thoughts, the ones everyone has when thinking about the limits of a life, or of beckoning death. Beth and Cassie were his world.

There was a light tap on the door, so gentle he assumed it was for a nearby office. A second tap followed nearly half a minute later. He swivelled his chair to face the opening door, and Nerida, nervous yet purposeful, entered, moved quickly across to him, leant forward, kissed him on the side of his half-open mouth, turned wordlessly and left, hurrying to the door, but not before a flushed neck betrayed any attempted composure.

Tom sat deep in thought for several minutes. The gum trees whispered outside, the wind caressing their branches. I know what I'll tell the dean, he said to himself.

Alias Stumpy

I first met Stumpy late one January as I was returning with a group of friends from having seen an exhibition of the Dutch Masters at the NSW Art Gallery. Strictly speaking, I wasn't returning with my friends, because I'd failed to collect my hat from the cloakroom, and had to return to collect it while they continued ahead.

The sky was louring, and distant rumbles of thunder and occasional flashes of lightning jagging the dimness promised something more forbidding. I hurried along Art Gallery Road and crossed College Street as gobs of rain began to fall, causing tiny explosions of steam to rise from the burning asphalt. It all seemed to heighten the supernatural aura of St Mary's Cathedral that towered on the corner.

Once inside the long tunnel that led to the underground St James railway station, I was safe, at least from the imminent storm.

'They're long gone,' a gentle voice said as I passed.

There were four homeless men who dossed down at night at a bend in the tunnel. We'd passed their belongings, the scattered, sad possessions of ill-fated lives when we'd arrived, but the approaching storm had brought the men back.

'I beg your pardon,' I stopped and answered, wondering why he assumed I was part of the group that had passed him earlier.

'Hey, Stumpy,' a voice called from across the tunnel, 'perhaps the kid can get us some dinner.'

The voice came from a dishevelled man of indeterminate years, dressed in stained army surplus, and speaking from a mouth of worn brown teeth with the front two missing. He sat on an open sleeping bag surrounded by a rucksack, a plastic water bottle, a rumpled towel, and empty take away containers. Sheets of cardboard were propped against the wall to protect him from night time cold, or immodesty.

One man sat on a torn rubber mattress, leaning forward to read a dog-eared book he'd placed on the ground. Another man, heavily bearded, was already asleep, mouth wide open, his flannel tracksuit pants hugging the underside of his large exposed buttocks.

'They'll have caught the four thirty-eight,' the man called Stumpy said. 'There's another one in twenty minutes.'

I'm not sure why I didn't hurry on like most people would have done out of embarrassment or uneasiness, counting their blessings. Perhaps the waiting time for the next train did not confer a reasonable excuse to do so. Instead I asked him where the name 'Stumpy' came from.

He couldn't recall. It had been with him for years, and nicknames emerge mysteriously, usually from light-hearted exchanges. His carried no literal meaning. Even sitting down, it was apparent that he was tall and slender. His hair was copious and white, and his clothes were clean if raffish. He sat on a cushion with his back to the tunnel wall. An old transistor radio and his rolled up sleeping bag were by his side. He appeared benign, even grandfatherly.

'And what's your name?' he asked.

Later I'd feel ashamed that I hesitated. And I'm sure he noticed it. But why be so wary?

'Paul Watson,' I eventually said.

'Paul Watson,' he repeated. 'And what do you do, Paul Watson?'

My life to date, though fortunate, hadn't been so much of a success story that I was self-conscious telling one less prosperous about it.

I explained that while most of my friends, the ones he'd seen in the tunnel before me, were at university, I had been working for a couple of years in a variety of different casual jobs to 'make ends meet'. 'My family aren't that well off,' I told him, feeling that he might appreciate hearing that life for others could also be a battle.

'I'm hoping to get into university this year,' I explained, realising that I had knelt down on the cold cement ground to talk to him. 'I had to send my CV and write a pleading letter saying why I deserve a place, because I'm a mature-age student. They only take a few of us. I'm pinning all my hopes on that letter,' I said and stopped, suddenly aware that I had said too much. He wouldn't be interested. He might even feel resentful, hearing the aspirations of one more fortunate, when he had little to aspire to himself.

'Stumpy,' I began. 'Can I call you Stumpy?'

'Everyone else does,' he answered.

'What did you do before you…well, before you came here?'

'A little bit of this and that,' he said evasively, looking directly at me. He had never once felt the need to lower his eyes.

Stumpy might well have told me his real name if he'd wanted to be called something less colloquial. And he obviously didn't want to talk about his earlier life. There might be no satisfaction for these men in detailing a stock market crash, broken marriages, retrenchment or substance abuse as explanations for their current plight.

'It's been nice to meet you, Paul Watson,' he said. 'Now you'd better hurry or you'll miss the train.'

*

A fortnight after my meeting with Stumpy, my mother was at the door when I returned home from one of my current jobs working in a local bookstore.

She was waving the letter in the air. 'Guess what this is?' she hailed excitedly.

I took the letter calmly, and sat in the family room, asking my mother about her day, deferring the inescapable reality with all the nonchalance that disguises real excitement.

'Aw, no,' I exclaimed, with mock disappointment, having finally opened the letter.

My mother's shoulders slumped.

'I'm in!' I shouted. 'I'm going to uni.'

My mother shared my excitement, and I knew my father would be pleased and relieved. Some years before, he had committed his savings to a business venture that involved selling laundry products door-to-door through a fleet of mini-mokes. The business failed, less from mismanagement than from the manager's absconding with everyone's money, and my father's savings were gone.

He'd felt guilty that I was unable to go to university directly from school, and was needed to work to help support my brothers and sisters. We weren't poor, but we certainly needed to tighten our belts. For the previous two years, I'd worked at several casual jobs, some concurrently, and my mother took in ironing. There was always food on the table and shoes on our feet, but my brothers and sisters had to be content with hand-me-downs.

That may be some explanation for my attraction to Mark. We'd been friends from school days, and he was the only son of Mr and Mrs Rupert Crossington. I don't think I felt envy, certainly not resentment, that Mark enjoyed the best of everything. Even at school, he had the top sporting equipment, and a new pair of expensive runners every few months. Our friendship was based on more than his good fortune, but the wealth of the Crossingtons did have a certain allure, even if it were only something to aspire to, a vision of my likely success from a university education, and at an age when status looms large.

He showed genuine pleasure at my acceptance into university, and invited me to stay with his family for a few days in February at their holiday home in Palm Beach before university started.

I had my own room in the Crossington holiday house while Mark shared a room with his new girlfriend. Celia was a fashion plate, very attractive in a baby doll way, expensively dressed whenever she ventured out, and without a hair out of place. Swimming was a challenge, but she didn't enter the surf beyond waist height. Mark was proud of the admiring looks she excited in her assortment of bikinis.

Dinners were formal affairs, reminiscent of Edwardian dining rooms. Mr Crossington sat at the head of the table, and his wife and Celia served. I'd get up to help, but Mark and his father sat quietly, or continued talking and didn't move.

'So what do you want to do when you finish university?' Mr. Crossington asked on my first night.

'I'm thinking of either social work or teaching,' I answered.

'Both noble professions,' he replied through a mouthful of rare beef, and with a meaningful glance at his wife. 'Of course, business and law is where the real money is.'

Celia, and Mrs Crossington, still a glamorous woman in her late forties, and considerably younger than her husband, had little to say throughout the meal, and I sensed that the Crossingtons senior were both pleased with their son's choice of girlfriend.

I enjoyed my stay, though at times I knew that Mark and Celia wanted to be alone, and felt like an interloper in the back seat of Mark's blue Porsche, a gift from his father, that he drove with abandon.

On my final night, Mr Crossington took us all to dinner at his club, and Mark lent me one of his silk Armani shirts and tie. I had to make do with my best pair of trousers.

'For heaven's sake, Paul,' Mark said light-heartedly, as the family waved me goodbye from the colonial veranda, and I opened the door of my old Datsun to return home, 'you really need to find yourself a new car. Not a good look at all.'

*

Unaware of the demands of tertiary education, I studied hard and passed my first year. I hadn't thought of Stumpy at all in that time, but my walk through the city streets to Wynyard station, after lunching with old friends, brought him to mind.

On many street corners, a homeless person was begging, often impeding the constant flow of people who waited to cross as the walk sign turned green. Most sat on the footpath with a grubby cap beside them, watching the passers-by. A few of them muttered entreaties that were not heard, or ignored. The majority, both men and women, and often quite young, did not show their faces, but knelt on the footpath, bent forward so that their heads touched the ground, and their faces were concealed. I cringe even now when I think of that image as it suggests a preparation for beheading. But the real pathos was the signs, scrawled on old cardboard, barely legible and often misspelt, giving bald explanations of misfortune.

Before I reached the station, I turned around with a sudden change of heart and retraced my steps, heading for St James station, knowing all the while that Stumpy might be long gone, or that he might be surly and not recognise me.

Neither he nor his companions were there, but his sleeping bag and radio were, so I waited, repeatedly walking from one end of the tunnel and back, bracing against the wind that must have been his constant enemy.

'Paul Watson.' He saw me first.

'You remembered,' I answered, unable to conceal my surprise and pleasure.

He had several days' growth of white stubble that, with his shock of unruly white hair, made him look considerably older than I remembered.

'Did you get into university?' he asked, as we headed slowly for the bend in the tunnel he regarded as home.

Somehow I sensed that he knew I had.

He unfolded his sleeping bag and we sat together, backs to the wall. He asked me about university and my exams, and I, without feeling any uneasiness, asked him what he did during the day, not that I received any satisfactory answer. Several people walked past, hurrying for the train, and looked at me curiously.

When one of his rowdy fellow dwellers arrived, a little the worse for wear, and stinking of spirits, I said goodbye, but walking only a little way along the tunnel and out of sight, I called home, asked if I could invite a relative stranger to dinner, and proceeded to tell my mother about Stumpy.

It was unusual for my father to be home at that hour in the afternoon, and I could hear them arguing as my mother passed on my message and her own pleas in instalments. My father said no, but after several minutes, my mother's reforming zeal defeated my father's innate suspicion, and a date was agreed upon.

I hurried back to tell Stumpy, but he was not impressed at all.

'No,' he said without hesitating. 'It's not my scene at all.'

I didn't want to embarrass him by insisting, when he didn't have suitable attire, or when he thought he mightn't smell like a rose. But I also thought that a satisfying dinner with people who cared, might be a step towards reclamation, even if I didn't know of what. I tried to convince him that my parents were not at all judgemental, and understood his situation.

We argued for a couple of minutes before, in mounting frustration, I issued an ultimatum. 'Stumpy,' I said, 'I'll be coming by next Thursday at five-thirty p.m., and I really hope you'll be ready to come with me. I'll be disappointed if you're not.'

He was ready. He'd soaked his hair and combed it into a semblance of wet order. He'd managed to shave, and was wearing an ill-fitting, old houndstooth coat. He followed me reluctantly to the train.

My mother had prepared a basic meal of meat and vegetables. 'Nothing too exotic,' she said. 'The poor man's stomach won't be able to cope.'

Stumpy removed his shoes at the door, and no one gave a hint of noticing the hole in his sock from which a big toe protruded.

The meal was a great success. My father was delighted by the questions that Stumpy asked about his work and investments, and it was apparent that my mother was really taken with him. She was overly attentive in her proffering of food and drink. Non-alcoholic cider of course.

I went back to St James with Stumpy, feeling he might be out of his comfort zone in travelling alone, and when I returned, my excited mother was waiting for me.

'Your dad and I have been discussing it, Paul, and we'd like Stumpy to come and live with us, at least for a week or two. We'll see how it works out. When will you be seeing him again?' She was full of plans. We could empty the spare room. Stumpy could have father's old but clean clothes. He might even get a job.

'No!' Stumpy said with convincing authority when I offered the invitation a few days later. I sat with him once again, our backs to the tunnel wall as people streamed by in the rush hour. We didn't say much. I quickly saw the futility of providing him with a litany of reasons as to why it would be a good thing.

'Thank your parents,' he finally said. 'You've all been very kind, and I do appreciate the offer. It may be hard for you to understand, but this is my life now, and I must live it as I see fit.'

*

It was several months before my work led me through St James tunnel to the station. Stumpy wasn't there. A neatly rolled sleeping bag was the only evidence of his meagre existence.

'He's in the hospital,' the bearded man opposite, the one known as 'Butcher', called out. 'Three of 'em, young bastards, set about kicking 'im. Cuts to his 'ead, broken ribs. I couldn't do nothin' because of me hernias.'

It wasn't difficult to find the hospital. Even though I only had a nickname, his appearance was unique. I was successful with the first call. The hospital didn't have a name for him either. Stumpy refused to give it, and there was no likelihood of Medicare or other health records The tag at bed's end in a busy public ward simply read 'Stumpy.' 'Name unknown' was written in smaller letters underneath.

I was saddened to see him like this. Apart from the cuts, and the bruises that had turned a purplish yellow, his cheeks were grey and sunken, and the light had gone from his eyes. He was in pain when he tried to move. Even though we didn't say much, I sensed that my presence was welcomed. Dialogue isn't the only form of communication.

'When you get out of here,' I asked as I readied to leave, 'I don't suppose you'd consider…'

He shook his head.

As I left the hospital and was walking down Victoria Street, I heard a voice call my name. It was Celia.

'What a surprise,' Mark said, vigorously shaking my hand, after I had been kissed on the cheek by Celia. 'Were you at the hospital? Not your mother or father, is it?' Mark was fond of them both.

'No, an old friend,' I replied. 'And where are you off to?'

They were both dressed with sartorial elegance, he in a navy suit, and she in a silver gown.

'It's some kind of business lunch,' Mark answered. 'Not exactly our cup of tea, but it's important to the old man. Important to be seen, you know. Can we drive you somewhere?'

I declined, needing the walk to clear my head, feeling strangely inadequate, so I was momentarily lost in my thoughts when the Porsche roared past.

*

For the previous year, the final one of my university studies, I had supplemented my reading of the sport pages with checking the obituaries on Saturday in *The Sydney Morning Herald*. A few of my friends had already lost parents prematurely, and I didn't want to miss the opportunity to offer my sympathy.

The list of deaths and funeral notices was sometimes accompanied by a more detailed obituary of a notable person. In December of that year, the photograph in one such account caught my eye, and I had to hold the paper up to the light to confirm my first impression. It was unmistakeably Stumpy, the picture of a younger Stumpy with iron-grey hair, looking immaculate in a pinstripe coat, but with the same benign expression.

I eagerly read the obituary.

Vale: Arthur Maurice Stephens. AM

Arthur Maurice Stephens was born in Melbourne in 1937 to Justice Malcolm and Lady Candice Stephens, and educated at Geelong Grammar School and Melbourne University, where he graduated with First Class Honours in Law and the university medal.

He worked tirelessly in prominent Melbourne and Sydney law firms as a champion of the disadvantaged and oppressed, before accepting the position of Chief Justice in 1987, where he gained a reputation for fair-mindedness and integrity.

Arthur was a well-known philanthropist, and a member or chairman of the boards of several charitable organizations. He was recognised with an Order of Australia in 1994.

He disappeared after his late retirement in 2007, having relinquished his legal and ex-officio roles.

His sole heir, Lady Stephens, passed away in 2009.

This account was followed by several glowing testimonials from former colleagues in the legal profession.

As I reread the obituary, images competed in my mind of Arthur Stephens in robes, looking regal at the bench, meticulous in his appraisal of evidence, and Stumpy sitting on his sleeping bag with his back to a cold and damp wall, nursing his only possession, an old transistor radio.

'I must live life as I see fit.' His words returned to me, and many questions curled around the images and wouldn't let go. Why do we choose the paths we do? Is there a trigger that makes us do so? Why would someone like Arthur Stephens opt for obscurity and privation?

*

I was left a very large sum of money in Stumpy's will. At first I thought of distributing some of it amongst Butcher and his mates, but for all I knew, Stumpy might have already made them beneficiaries. Or perhaps he'd decided that, like him, their lives were committed to other irrevocable paths.

I didn't want people to know of my good fortune, not that I was uneasy about hangers-on. I felt that, in some odd way, it would be a violation of the private and special relationship Stumpy and I had shared. Perhaps some of Arthur's renowned discretion had rubbed off on me.

But people did find out, I don't know how, and for a month, the calls kept coming. A few disguised covetousness with an overly enthusiastic camaraderie. Most were genuine expressions of goodwill.

Mark and Celia were certainly genuine in their congratulations. Fitting reward for such hard work, they both said in their different ways. Of course, they were referring to my study at university and my helping at home that had nothing to do with Stumpy's largesse. I couldn't help but wonder if I were now seen as a more compatible companion.

'Well, Paul,' Mark enthused, slapping me on the shoulder, 'you'll be able to buy yourself a decent car now.'

I looked at him and said nothing.

The Weight of Feeling

This story isn't so much about me as another, though I have a small part to play as a confidant, and as someone who may have influenced some of the action. I'm fortunate that Troy Douglas, the subject of the tale, laid his heart open to me. I say 'fortunate' because men of my generation are notoriously poor at revealing much of themselves, particularly their emotions. But sometimes the emotion is so great, it's hard to contain. This was the case with Troy, at least in the early days of our friendship. So I'll try to tell his story with as much fidelity as I can, bearing in mind that any reality must be refracted through the eyes of the teller, and that our childhood language might be reported in a more adult way.

My name is Neil Henry, forty years of age, and I was part of a large family that lived in a well-to-do suburb of Adelaide. When I first met Troy in primary school, after our family's arrival in the area, he lived in a large liver brick house a street away, so we began our friendship as walking companions to school. Troy was an only child whereas I had brothers and sisters.

But our friendship was more than circumstantial. We not only shared interests, we were able to talk about the feelings and the anxieties that we couldn't share with our other peers who would never admit to anything unmanly or 'girly', yet were unconvincing in their attempts to bluff.

We got on well with the others, though, swapping cigarette cards, playing marbles in the dirt playground at lunchtime, refusing to dob on mates, and performing well enough in the rough and tumble games that operate to determine a pecking order among primary-aged boys.

My father was a teacher of science at the local secondary school, and Troy's father worked in the public service, though Troy was uncertain of what exactly he did. My mother had her hands full looking after the needs of a husband and five children. Troy's mother worked part-time in a secretarial firm.

How often do stories have a definite beginning and end? Perhaps a starting point is the time I asked Troy about a large purplish bruise on his cheek and a half closed and weeping black eye. Even at the tender age of ten, I didn't believe the dodge about walking into a door. And he knew I didn't believe it.

It was probably that realisation, and our sworn pact about honesty with each other, that led us to his bedroom that afternoon after school on one of his mother's working days. Once inside, the defences relaxed and he began to cry. I seem to remember that I did too. His pain was mine too even though I had no understanding of the cause.

That's when he told me the beginning of the story. The rest that followed over the next few years involved variations on a theme.

*

Troy's father had come home at eight p.m. the night before, reeking of alcohol, spoiling for a fight, and offering no apology for being late. This wasn't the first time, Troy reported, so both he and his mother had cause for alarm.

'Where's my bloody dinner,' he called without a word of welcome or inquiry. 'It's not bloody much for a man to expect.'

'It's in the oven, Colin,' his wife tried to appease. 'I'll get it for you,' and she hurried to the oven and carried the plate to the table.

'It's bloody dried up,' he roared. 'Do you really expect me to eat that? I want a decent meal when I get home after a hard day's work.'

'We always eat at seven, Colin.' His wife tried to sound as reasonable as possible, though Troy could tell she was frightened.

He heard the resounding crack of the slap across his mother's face.

She stood still, not daring to speak or retreat, not even raising her hands to her trembling face as the tears coursed down her cheeks.

'That'll bloody teach you to be smart and answer back,' his father growled. 'Stop blubbering, woman,' he warned, but his mother couldn't.

'I couldn't help it,' Troy told me. 'It was so unfair. I charged at him. I don't know what I had in mind. He'd really hurt Mum. I just wanted it all to stop. But I didn't get a chance to do any damage even if I'd planned to.'

Troy was thrown backwards by the blow that landed on the side of his face. This time it was with a closed fist. It felt as if his head was about to explode. He couldn't move his jaw, and lay on the floor, senseless for a few seconds before his father started cursing. This time with the 'f' word, Troy reported.

'I'll teach you to meddle,' he shouted. 'You're just like your mother,' and he made his way towards Troy, who had already scrambled to his feet and started to run. His father was close behind, removing the heavy studded belt from his trousers. The air stank of alcohol.

Troy was terrified, and could hear his mother screaming, sobbing and panting heavily to find breath as his father advanced. Troy headed for the stairs. There was nowhere else to go. The front door was closed and he wouldn't have had time to open it before his father struck. His bedroom was at the top of the stairs, not that it would offer much relief. It could only delay the inevitable.

He cleared the first three stairs in one jump, and heard his father fall with another volley of curses. The removal of his belt had caused his trousers to gather around his ankles.

Troy raced into his bedroom and closed the door, expecting his father any second. The door couldn't be locked anyway, so it was only temporary relief. He was terrified as he ran to the walk-in robe, concealed himself as best he could behind his clothes, and closed the door.

'Neal,' Troy stopped the account. 'I'll never tell anyone this as long as I live, but I know I can trust you.'

'Of course, Troy,' I must have said. 'Your secrets will always be safe with me,' and his next admission was for me, at that stage in my life, the most poignant of all.

'I wet myself,' he said with his eyes lowered.

I didn't know what to say, unschooled as I was at that age to deal with another's pain. Such an accident was a source of great shame for a ten-year-old boy.

After half a minute of silence, he continued. 'I don't know how long I stayed in the wardrobe. It might have been a couple of hours. My cheek was throbbing, and I could feel the skin pinching and drawing like a curtain around my eye. I didn't know if the wetness was water or blood, and couldn't see in the dark. With every little noise, a creaking of floorboards or a settling in the walls, I thought he was coming, but I guess he went back to eat what he could of his dinner. The shouting subsided after a while but I daren't get out of the wardrobe, even though the small of naphthalene was making me feel sick.

'After a long while, I could hear them in their bedroom next door to mine. The bed was jumping on the floor every second or two, the mattress was squeaking, and my mother was calling out and crying. "You're hurting me, Colin. Please stop. No, no."

'I couldn't hear what he was saying. It was more like a low growl. It all stopped suddenly, and there was a deathly silence.

'When it had been quiet for some time, I crept out. I didn't want to wake him and remind him. I took off my wet shorts that had begun to stink, but wasn't game to go to the bathroom to wash them. My bedside clock said twelve o'clock when I went to bed.'

It was to become a familiar scenario for the morning after.

Troy's father did apologise to him, but down played the seriousness of what he had done. 'Sorry about hitting you, Troy,' he said, as though it were some minor transgression. 'Lost my cool for a moment there.' He didn't say anything about hitting Mrs Douglas. Perhaps what happened in the bedroom the night before was his warped gesture of apology to her, a peace offering of sorts.

His mother kept watching him throughout the family's silent breakfast, wanting to treat his swollen cheek and his closed and weeping eye, but not wanting to draw her husband's attention to it.

'Better tell them at school you walked into a door,' his father said. 'High five, mate,' he said light-heartedly, holding up his flattened hand in salute. And kissing his wife, he left for work.

It didn't escape Troy's understanding that his father was remorseful, but trying to diminish the significance of what had happened with false cheer. It was obvious that he was anxious to escape the house, and the scene of his abusing as soon as possible. As far as he was concerned, time would be the great healer.

'Why couldn't he apologise as if he really meant it?' Troy asked his mother. 'Will it ever be any different?'

'He really can be very kind, Troy.' His mother felt the need to defend her husband, and she held Troy in a long embrace. Her cheeks were wet.

*

In our late primary and early secondary school years, Troy seemed to be more withdrawn. He didn't arrive at school with any obvious injuries although, on a couple of occasions, he seemed to be walking more gingerly. I didn't ask about it because I knew it was a sensitive topic, and it might upset him. He'd talk if he needed to.

His usual *joie de vivre* was replaced with lethargy, though natural ability enabled him to succeed in his studies. In those years, he only referred to his father's abuse three times, not with as much graphic detail as before, though I suspect it was ongoing.

'Has your mum ever thought about leaving him,' I had the nerve to ask once, 'and taking you with her?'

Troy was silent for a while. Home was all we knew in those tender years, and we were fearful of relinquishing such a foundation even if the bedrock was crumbling.

'She's never mentioned it,' he answered.

Of course we didn't understand then the financial implications, or even the notion that love was still possible even for the victim of abuse.

In our first year of secondary school, Troy's father took us to Sydney and to the Royal Easter Show.

'You can say you're doing something else,' Troy said apologetically, 'but he insists on taking me, and wants me to bring a friend. Perhaps it's his way of saying sorry.'

I knew Troy would be anxious not to be left alone with his father, and I wasn't that noble that I wanted to miss the opportunity.

It was my first time in a plane, and we stayed in a motel, going to the show on three different days, seeing the exhibits of produce, the animals, the dog show, and the car and motorbike stunt driving. Even though my parents were generous in supplying money, Troy's father bought me show bags, and paid for our evening meals.

My original concern about his temper, and the possibility of also becoming a victim of abuse, was short-lived. He treated me with the concern and affection I was accustomed to from my own father.

To my shame, looking back, I began to wonder if Troy's descriptions of his father's abuse were exaggerated. In our youth, we often describe things in extremes. It's the nature of childish emotion, and it's only with maturity that issues are weighed more critically and some things are seen to be problematic.

Troy could see what I was thinking, and it must have saddened him, but he didn't say anything.

*

As adults, we say in many clichéd ways that there is little poetic justice in the world, and that fate doesn't seem to strike equitably. As the years flew by, I felt increasingly fortunate about my own family life, particularly when I heard about the tragedy in Troy's. There were five children in our family, and none had suffered beyond the bumps and cuts of rugby, or adolescent broken hearts. And yet Troy now had another cross to bear.

Once we'd left school, we'd taken different paths. We attended the same university, but enrolled in different faculties, and he was a part-time student. But we did keep in touch, and that's how I learnt about the accident.

Troy was only eighteen when his father had fallen from an upstairs window onto rocks below while trying to repair a wooden shutter. He had died instantly. It was a working day for Troy's mother, so Troy had returned from university to find the body.

'What was it like?' I asked, wondering if I sounded ghoulish, but Troy didn't mind.

He needed to talk. For him, it was the incantation that follows bereavement. 'It was strange,' he answered. 'This man I was so frightened of for all those years, lying on the rocks with the blood pooling around his head, he looked like…like something pathetic, so insignificant.'

The funeral was well attended by his work colleagues and his contacts at the soccer club. Numerous of them spoke, eulogising his practical joking and sense of humour, applauding his efficiency at work, and praising him as a devoted husband and father. 'A really good bloke' was the consensus.

Troy remained expressionless throughout with his head bowed. His mother repeatedly dabbed at her eyes with a sodden handkerchief.

He qualified for university accommodation shortly after that, and his mother moved away. I've heard recently that she remarried shortly afterwards.

*

Close same-sex bosom friendships typically give way to the demands of new families. At the age of twenty-six, I married Shannon, a girl I met at university, training to be a teacher. We were fortunate enough to purchase a small house not far from her parents in a nearby suburb to my own family home.

Troy married Natalie six months later, a girl we both knew from our secondary school days. They bought a unit several suburbs away.

Each of us was best man at the other's wedding, and while we tried to meet every month or two for catch-up, the birth of children for both of us meant that the month or two became a year or two, and when the children attended school, our contact stopped.

It was six years later, as my story heads towards its conclusion, that I heard of Troy again. Shannon's brother is a policeman, and because he'd attended our wedding, he'd also met Troy. He had disturbing news for Shannon, who passed it on to me.

Natalie had taken out an apprehended violence order against Troy due to his violence towards her and the two children. Police were considering whether he should be formally charged.

'I don't believe it,' I said. 'Not after what he went through as a kid.'

'I didn't at first,' Shannon replied. 'It is hard to believe, but apparently there's sufficient physical evidence…weals, bruising and the like.'

I arranged a meeting with Natalie. I thought it best to hear her story before I confronted Troy. We met at a restaurant and were fortunate to find a corner booth. She was obviously distressed, and I knew this wouldn't be easy for her.

'I know,' she began before I'd said a word, anticipating my near disbelief. 'Who'd have thought it. Troy. Domestic violence.' And as if she might have contributed to his behaviour, 'I've been a good wife, Neal, and a good mother.'

She explained his mood swings in detail, one moment attentive and loving, and the next belligerent and violent. But most often, he was devoid of any emotion, taciturn and without expression. He didn't hit the children, but he was verbally abusive. He did hit her.

'It's hard enough for me to endure,' she began to cry. 'But Phoebe wets the bed every night now, and Jack suffers from terrible anxiety.'

'I'll speak to him, Natalie. Perhaps he'll listen to me.'

'No, Neal! I appreciate your concern, but I'm not going to be one of these women who give their husbands a second, third and fourth chance. I won't allow my children to suffer a moment longer.'

Divorce proceedings were already under way, and I thought it best to wait for Troy to approach me. He might not be pleased by my interference. Or he might crave understanding rather than criticism. I mightn't condone his actions, but I could be a sympathetic ear.

*

His message came by phone out of the blue a few months ago. He wanted to talk and the phone wasn't personal enough. His voice was quiet and lacking any pleasure or expression. I thought he might have been a little more enthusiastic about making contact.

I had heard from Natalie that the divorce was finalised years ago, custody wasn't contested, and he was living alone in a run-down office behind a cobbler's shop. He had left a secure job, and was making do with part-time work.

He shook my hand when we met the following Saturday, but his deadpan look didn't alter. 'Do you remember our pact back in primary school?' he began so softly I had to lean forward to hear. 'Complete honesty.'

'I remember very well,' I said, and was about to remind him of our undertaking to keep secrets, but he continued.

'I can't feel, Neal,' he said. 'I know I hurt Natalie and the kids. I know I was doing to them what was done to me.'

He stopped, and I wasn't going to make the mistake of interrupting.

'People out there,' and he gestured with a wave of the hand, 'get excited, they squeal with delight, they're moved by each other's plight, they experience grief, quiet contentment, they're disappointed when their expectations aren't met, they're moved to tears by a God they worship, they nurse fantasies and make plans for rosy futures, they even fall in love.'

He stared at me blankly.

'I don't feel any of it. It's almost as if we have a finite amount of emotion, like a bucket full, and when it all leaks out of the bucket, it's gone, and there's nothing left.'

He sat in silence for a full minute, and I felt it was time to challenge.

'Doesn't friendship involve a feeling?' I asked. 'Something warm, or at least positive?'

'You're a friend,' he said, 'because you listen, and you've always made an effort to understand. There's a gratitude of sorts, but don't ask me for more than that, Neal. I'm inured to the claims of emotion.'

There was another long silence, and Troy was looking into the distance.

'I killed him, you know.'

'I beg your pardon,' I said, only half comprehending.

'My father, I killed him. I thought you knew.'

'No, I…I…'

'I pushed him out the window. I was home earlier from uni than I said. He didn't see me. Didn't make a sound on the way down. I looked out the window and saw him on the rocks below. I walked down slowly, no hurry. He wasn't dead, trying to say something but no sound came out.'

I don't think he wanted to go on talking. He was staring towards the window, and I was lost for words. What do you say to someone after an admission like that? And especially when he was quite unmoved by it. So we shook hands and I left.

It had been a meeting of several long silences. He knew his secret was safe with me. Was our childhood pact the reason for this late revelation? I'd never know. I never saw him again.

*

It was a few weeks before I heard of his suicide. The news came from Shannon's brother, the policeman. It must have happened days after we'd spoken, and I tried to imagine how he faced the end. It would certainly have been calm and measured.

Was his admission to me about his father a gesture of goodbye, a statement made not from guilt but simply to set the record straight? Perhaps a final endorsement of the honesty that was so important to both of us?

Shannon held me in a tight embrace when I first heard the news, without saying a word. She didn't have to. We stood that way for at least a minute.

'At least my bucket's full,' I eventually said, releasing her, and she looked at me curiously.

Absence Makes the Heart

She was coming home. The crew on the red-eye special from Heathrow to Sydney were opening the window blinds, and even though it was early morning and an hour from Sydney, the fluffy clouds were dazzling white with sun. The light filled the plane as one shade after another was opened. It woke several passengers, who drowsily moved their makeshift pillows, looked towards the toilets to see if a green light indicated a vacancy, or stood to find some morning essential from the overhead lockers. Others, who had scarcely slept at all, kept glazed eyes glued to the television screens in front of them. A few slept on oblivious.

'Only an hour or two now,' the man sitting beside her said, rubbing the stubble on his chin. 'Can't wait.'

'Anything special you can't wait for?' Melanie replied to make conversation, and thought she might have been presumptuous. She felt a little furry-headed from a jostled sleep.

'Gloria,' the man answered. 'I really missed her. A fortnight away, and it seemed like forever.' He stood from his aisle seat to reach for his hand luggage. 'Better have a shave.' Gloria was probably meeting him at the airport.

They'd had sporadic conversation throughout the flight, the pleasantries assumed on boarding and just as suddenly relinquished with landing.

'Anyone special waiting for you?' he asked, but not taking much notice.

'Yes,' Melanie answered, but showed no inclination to elaborate.

The man was too absorbed to inquire further.

When he'd gone to the toilets, Melanie took a pile of letters from her hand luggage, annotations of a tender yet recently troubled past, giving them their sentient freedom from the rubber band that balled them together. She riffled through them, finding an early one. 'My Darling Melanie,' it began,

As I was walking along our special beach yesterday at twilight, that time when the day is somehow freed of tension, I saw a couple lying in the sand, moving as one in age-old show, if you know what I mean. It was like a production, a cast of two, lit dimly by a watery rose, and orchestrated by the waves. And I was the audience.

I had to pass close by, and felt, I don't know why, that I was the one who'd been found out. I was embarrassed and resentful. There was a creamy moon that lit a thigh that curled, snakelike in the dying light. And I passed unseen.

I've never longed for anyone as I did for you then. I felt so desolate, all by myself beneath the brightening stars. It's only been a little over a week, and missing you is painful. Not sure how I'm going to cope with the weeks and months ahead. Please write soon and tell me you feel the same.

That was sometimes typical of his prose when he'd strive for poetic effect. Melanie read a second letter, one of many, written only ten days ago:

Dearest Melanie,

I can't tell you how pleased I am that our trial separation is nearing an end. It's been agony for me, and while I hope it has not been the same for you, I'd like to think that I have been sorely missed. I've been crossing off the days on the doggie calendar on the kitchen door. Kaiser helps me.

I've kept the place neat and tidy, and even painted the spare room in that pale avocado colour you showed me on the paint chart.

Can you give me any more insight into how you're feeling? Do you yearn to return to those great times we used to share together? Every night I go to bed and nurse one of those memories, savouring it like one of those Red Tulip cherry liqueur chocolates you love. More a selected recall before I fall asleep than an actual dream.

I love you, Mel, and can't wait till I hold you again. A huge hug from me, and a big lick from Kaiser.

Your ever-loving husband.

The man returned from the toilet smelling of aftershave, and began filling in documents for customs.

'A trial separation,' she'd called it. That's the name it was always given. She remembered Royce's face when she told him. He was crushed.

'Is there no other way?' he managed to say after a minute's tearful silence, the family room palpable with pain.

'Three months,' she'd said. 'It's our only chance, Royce,' she continued gently, mindful of his hurt. 'There's a great deal I have to think about. I can't do it here, and I can't do it overnight.'

It wasn't negotiable. She'd already arranged to live for three months with her sister in Brighton. She'd even arranged some part-time work. She'd been looking forward to a change of scene, wondering if it would also mean a change of heart. She was gone a few days later, insisting that she alone catch a taxi to the airport, and leaving Royce and Kaiser sitting together mournfully in the family room.

'A trial separation,' he reflected, as he heard the taxi depart on the gravel driveway. The idea of a trial implied undergoing a test, answering to some sort of accountability. It seemed to him that the only protagonists in such a trial were time and circumstance. And they were fickle allies.

The crew was given landing instructions by the captain, and the plane began its slow descent. Behind that last letter was her rough copy of the one she'd sent in reply. She wouldn't normally make a copy but it was important to convey the right message.

Dear Royce,

I've had an interesting and often enjoyable time in Brighton, and have wondered how you're getting along. Not just eating junk food! I hope Kaiser is looking after you. Give him a pat from me.

I 'd like to stay a little longer, and Pru would like me to as well, but I did say three months, and must be true to my word. I leave here on the sixteenth.

I'm not sure where I stand, or is it sit, with things between us at the moment. I thought I would see things with greater clarity when away from them. Perhaps I was mistaken. My return, and seeing you again, may make things clearer for me.

Please don't come to the airport. I'll contact you soon after I arrive. Till then, keep well.

Melanie.

*

'So why isn't it working?' Veronica asked. She'd been a friend with Melanie for many years, and no subject was taboo for them, no enquiry deemed in poor taste.

They were sipping cappuccinos in their usual meeting spot.

'You know, Vee, I'm not sure,' Melanie answered. 'I know the list of adjectives applied to these things is endless, usually epithets on the graves of dead relationships. And the words are *ex post facto*, applied when it's all over to justify someone's decision, when the words weren't even thought of when things weren't going well. We have this need to tag things.

'Then what are some of the adjectives?' Veronica asked after the several seconds she needed to take this in. 'Words he might apply to you, and words you might apply to him.'

'He loves me to a fault,' Melanie replied, more with concern than satisfaction. As for words, he might call me practical, pragmatic, possibly unromantic. I think he might have been disappointed sometimes that I didn't share his dreams.'

'And what words, what adjectives, might you use to describe him?'

'Part of the problem, Vee, is that he's a really good man. The adjectives I might use aren't negatives at all. Most people would think of them as positives…. words like visionary, idealistic, romantic.'

'But those qualities could be annoying, right?' Veronica challenged.

'I'll give you an example,' Melanie answered, 'Royce has always had this thing about boats. You know that. Of course we couldn't afford one. I'd see him some nights on the front porch, leaning against the rail, except for him it isn't a porch with hydrangeas around but a boat in the sea with the spray blowing needles to ginger his face. It's not just my imagination, because he keeps telling me to see it like he does. One night he came inside to make love, but I knew his heart wasn't there, so how do you think I should feel when a boat he can only invent in his mind is his passion, more important than I am?'

'Phew,' Veronica exhaled. 'What did you do?'

'I joined him on the porch one night, and asked him if we could both sail away together. I've rarely seen him so happy. He raced inside to get his windcheater. I held his arm against the buffeting wind and tugged at the wheel while we steered the front porch by the stars.'

'That's just so wonderful, Mel,' Veronica said emotionally after a long silence. 'How could he possibly think of you as not being romantic? And isn't that something you could keep doing…living his fantasies with him?'

They drank their coffees, lost in their own thoughts for several minutes before Veronica spoke.

'He wasn't very happy then when you told him you were going to England?'

'It was terrible.' Melanie was close to tears recalling the talk that had come as a complete surprise to Royce. 'I don't think it's working, do you, I asked, knowing he'd never agree, that he'd be astonished. I don't think it's working for me, Royce. I didn't want to sound too definite or final about it all, and I was losing conviction seeing his pain. What can I do, he asked plaintively like a little child who wants nothing more than to please, and at that moment I wanted to tell him to forget everything I'd just said. Give him a hug.'

'But you didn't.'

'No, I said something trite like the problems between people – no, that's not it. I said that what makes people unhappy can't always be changed by actions. It's often simply who they are.'

*

She insisted on taking a taxi to the airport. Didn't want any fraught goodbyes. She sat in the departure lounge feeling half-real, questioning what she was doing. It had been years since she'd seen her sister, but she couldn't muster enthusiasm. The world wasn't full of exciting possibilities. It was pressing against her, weighing her down.

She watched the threads of cloud floating across a sky struggling for colour, observed the landing planes mope home like scolded dogs with noses to the scent. Some waiting passengers dozed, and others read. Families chatted till, clichés spent, their thoughts attenuated to fairy breath.

Her flight number was eventually called for boarding. For Melanie, the world was mutating to endless uncertainties.

It wasn't a comfortable trip, but her sister did all she could to restore her spirits, and the structure of the family's life, and a prearranged job in the university library, gave her purpose and pleasure. She ran each morning, bought a leotard and went to yoga classes once a week, collected her sister's young children from school on the odd occasion, and shared the cooking responsibilities. It didn't take long to settle in.

She'd only been there for four days when the first of many letters arrived. It must have been written the day she left:

My dear Melanie,

Forgive me but I'm torn between the need to write and giving you the space I think you need. I suppose my way is to talk it all through, whatever 'it all' is, rather than retreat, but I have to respect your decision.

You'll laugh when I say I'm missing you when it's only been an hour since you left, but that's probably when it hits hardest, and the realisation comes home. Will it become any easier? Will acceptance help? I rather think not.

Mel, I don't want to pressure you, but if you could tell me how I could change, make a list, even if it's only a couple of things to work on while you're away. I can't make any promises, but I'll certainly try.

I hope you had a comfortable trip. [The next sentence was heavily crossed out. One can only surmise why.] Say hello to Pru from me. Kaiser sends his love.

You're my life Mel, R xx

Melanie was not pleased to receive the letter. Not so soon. But she knew Royce was hurting, and through no real fault of his own. And she did have responsibilities towards him, even if she had made it clear that she needed her space. So she waited for a week and wrote back, a restrained letter thanking him for his well wishes, and telling him she was having valuable reflection time, and that it was too early to be making a list of the sort he wanted. It ended with an appeal for patience.

Time dragged for Royce, a procession of near endless days to face an achromatic world, to force himself to leave the bed and room that had grown with them, to hear the dawn's mournful lament of the crows with their human sounding fall, and to brave the innocent 'Where's Mel?' questions.

*

When Melanie arrived back after her three months in England, she felt things were different yet the same, and knew that the feeling was simply the mind making the transition back to the familiar. Thankfully, Royce, as requested, wasn't there to meet her, and then she realised that she'd given him the wrong date of return. She was a day early and Royce would be at work.

She rang Veronica from the airport, and they met an hour later at a café not far from their homes.

'So tell me,' Veronica began as soon as they'd hugged and admired each other's rude good health. 'What have you decided? Is it any clearer?' She felt the indecision in Melanie, and noted the hint of a frown.

'Still doubts, I suppose, Vee,' Melanie replied. 'But Royce is a good man and he's done nothing wrong.'

Veronica wanted to say that continuing in a relationship wasn't simply a matter of a partner not being culpable, but didn't.

'Anyway, any decision I make now isn't set in cement,' Melanie continued. 'For the time being, I'll go on as if everything is all right. It's important now that I make a real effort to make it work.'

Veronica was less certain of her friend's wisdom. She was still uncertain after three months, but she knew that Melanie would never deliberately hurt Royce. Besides, it wasn't her place to challenge. Melanie had made her decision.

Kaiser was there to meet her when she let herself in at home, at first with a growl, until recognition took over and he leapt on her, furiously wagging his tail. Royce had been true to his word. The place was in immaculate order, the bed was made, and photographs of her still enjoyed their prominent place on the dressing table.

She unpacked and, as she'd missed breakfast on the plane, made herself a salad. Royce must have bought salad things in anticipation. It was still late morning and she decided to go on a run.

Unlike the busy streets of Brighton where runners had to dodge cars and wait at crossings, the roads near Melanie's house were rarely used, and wound through bush that at different times of the year was in full flower. She'd missed her runs here.

She'd been running for several minutes, filling her lungs with the scented air, and hearing the birdsong, when she saw something ahead in the slight ditch at the side of the road. At first she thought it was rubbish or a discarded overcoat, but as she approached, she could see that it was a man.

He wasn't old. About her own age. Dressed in professional-looking black nylon running garb, lying helplessly on his back, making no effort to move, and in obvious pain.

Melanie sprinted to his side, saw him clutching at his chest, and instantly phoned 000 on her mobile that she took everywhere in the case of emergencies.

She made him comfortable as best she could, sitting in the hollow at the side of the road and resting his head on her lap, stroking his forehead, watching his startled eyes questioning, imploring help, and holding him like a child.

She'd later try to remember what she said to him. Probably the soothing things you might say to an injured child: 'You're going to be fine', 'Try to remain calm', 'The ambulance is on its way.' He tried to speak but couldn't, and there in a baked clay hollow with the singing of birds, and a profusion of sunlit yellow pellets of wattle against a ming blue sky, she sensed acceptance birthing in his eyes, and felt the dying flutter.

It was only a minute before the ambulance arrived, but it was too late. After the ambulance men's confirming check, and the telltale exchange of looks, they showed more concern about her than the man for whom there was no need for any further intervention. She'd later learn his name was Derek.

'Can we drive you home, miss?' they asked with obvious concern, but Melanie declined despite their protests of her having received a shock.

She continued sitting in the hollow for what must have been hours, sometimes clasping drawn-up knees, sometimes lying prostrate against the warm clay, feeling its honest and epicene embrace. She imagined Royce, probably at home now, being delighted by her early return. Perhaps being encouraged by it. He'd kiss her, gently, careful not to force anything, showing his pleasure at seeing her again, mix her a brandy and dry, her favourite drink, as she, a distant look in her eyes, prepared to say a final goodbye. Three months changed nothing. A few seconds did.

*

Melanie was right with her prediction. Royce was surprised and pleased by her early return, and practised a polite restraint, kissing her and holding her briefly. He even offered to make her the brandy and dry.

Both of them thought it indelicate to launch into their feelings about the trial separation, so the talk centred on her time at Brighton and his time at home. She asked after the meals he'd cooked, and enquired about Kaiser and the neighbours. He asked about how she'd managed with Pru and the family, and about her job in the university library.

'Did you get all my letters?' he asked, not at first realising that he had initiated the real purpose of the reunion. It was a pointless question too, unless she knew exactly how many he'd sent.

Melanie drew breath. It was time. Time for what she had feared for months, yet no longer did. 'My purpose in going away…' she began.

'No, let me go first,' Royce interrupted.

Melanie felt that the rug had been pulled from under her feet. She wanted to give her decision without having to listen to Royce's pleadings. Their exchange would no longer be restrained, perhaps not even polite. It would be highly emotion-charged. She would have to endure Royce's protests of all he had done to improve himself. Her decision coming after that would cast her permanently in the role of villain. Still, she reasoned, he would probably want his say anyway. Was there any way to avoid it?

'I've given it a great deal of thought,' he resumed and paused, watching for her reaction. 'And I think it would be better for us both if we went our separate ways.' After a few seconds, he added, 'I'm quite sure of it.'

A few minutes later, Melanie, still in her sports gear, running along the same road as before, reached the spot she'd sat in only an hour or two before. The sun was setting, and colouring the wattle a burnished gold. The birds were silent. She sat in the clayey hollow, looking up at the sky, shaking her head, and the tears rolled down her cheeks.

Keeping Memories Alive

It's often said that the sum is greater than the parts. So it is with a description of my friend Owen. Long eyelashes and cherubic lips in a man might be regarded as effeminate. He wasn't. His eyes were dark, almost black, giving him a brooding look, and he had a mop of black hair that he had to repeatedly shake from his eyes with a toss of the head, hair that hung over his collar. It's just as well he never met my aunt. She'd have headed straight to the scissors drawer. Handsome? That was the consensus among the girls.

My aunt might have needed to access more than scissors, because Owen's lack of conventionality showed itself in raffish clothes and questionable manners. It wasn't that he was rude or trying to score points against a stylised world. It was simply that conformity didn't matter to him.

It's not surprising that people were intrigued by our relationship. Even my name, Charles, smacks of old-world conservatism. I conform. I believe in tradition and established procedures. Appearances and the social niceties are important to me. On several occasions we were greeted as 'the odd couple', and I'm convinced that everyone who knew us thought so.

We were classmates at school, where he roasted me for my slavish observance of the school culture, calling me 'a goody-goody', and I warned him of the perils of not conforming. We maintained our friendship beyond school even though we took different paths. Perhaps he saw in me the orthodoxy he couldn't own, and I saw in him a freedom from convention, a need to break free. I studied political science at university, while he became a student at the National Institute for Dramatic Art.

In my first year at university I attended a concert with my sister Elizabeth, a tall, willowy blonde two years older than me and with startlingly good looks that accounted for a self-assurance that bordered on cockiness. Ever since she was a young girl, Elizabeth had clear ideas of what she wanted, unusual for one so young, and was single-minded in her pursuit of them.

I became aware of Owen that night in another section of the auditorium, looking towards us on several occasions. I waved once with no reaction. In our conversation the following day, I learned that his interest wasn't so much in attracting my attention, as in admiring Elizabeth. Discretion, perhaps reluctance to appear too eager, demanded understatement, at least at first.

'That was a nice girl I saw you with yesterday,' Owen said casually.

There may have been a flicker of relief when I told him it was my sister.

Over the next two weeks, Owen saw Elizabeth from afar on a number of occasions, usually with me, and it soon became apparent that he was smitten. For one so far outside the social norms, and a student of the theatre, it may seem surprising that Owen wasn't more direct in revealing his feelings, but he was painfully shy, and probably unsure of how to behave.

As I considered how to arrange a meeting between Owen and Elizabeth, the decision was made for me.

'Your friend Owen,' Elizabeth said in her typically direct way, 'I'd like you to introduce me, and include me in whatever you do.'

'Gladly, sis,' I replied, careful to avoid light-hearted references to lovebirds. She wouldn't have liked that.

Elizabeth read my matchmaking thoughts and was quick to dispel them. 'His father's head of Collins,' she said, and chose not to react to my sudden disappointment.

Elizabeth had made it known for years that she wanted to move into publishing from the drudgery of her current secretarial position. She was not only drawn by the work, she had aspirations to be published herself. Collins was the most prestigious publishing company in the state. Knowing the single-minded way she pursued her objectives, I was concerned for Owen. I didn't want him to be simply a pawn in my sister's game.

'Elizabeth,' I said, 'Owen really likes you. A lot!' I felt the need to add.

'I know,' Elizabeth said matter-of-factly. 'I've seen the way he looks at me. So the mission is half accomplished.'

'I hope you aren't planning to string him along till you get what you want, and then drop him.' I was feeling annoyed by her arrogance.

'We'll see what happens,' Elizabeth answered. 'Who knows? It's early days, and you, my dear little brother, can make sure I see plenty of Owen, and say nothing about Collins.'

*

Wattamolla beach and picnic ground is a beautiful and isolated spot in the Royal National Park near Wollongong. A calm lagoon flows to the ocean and is ideal for swimming and snorkelling. Groves of cabbage tree palms offer protection from the sun and prying eyes, and there are several coastal bush walks. It was here that I invited Owen and Elizabeth.

While I was host of the occasion, I soon became aware that Elizabeth was orchestrating the day, beginning with our lying on our towels in the sun, with her pretending not to notice the effect on Owen of her honey- coloured figure in a red bikini.

Owen obviously admired her, yet probably thought it indelicate to say so. At first he seemed to be almost tongue-tied, giving brief answers to the variety of interested questions Elizabeth asked to draw him out, but as he became more comfortable, the conversation flowed. My own contribution was the rare flattering comment about each of them, offered for the benefit of the other.

Elizabeth handled the situation with consummate ease. 'Come on,

Owen,' she called, climbing to her feet, and reaching out to take his hand. 'Let's swim around to that rock. Don't worry about Charles,' she added when she saw Owen look to me. 'He's an old stick-in-the mud,' and she knelt down and kissed my forehead, in case Owen thought she might be serious.

I watched them run hand in hand to the water's edge and dive as one, striking out towards the rock. I knew then that I'd chosen our first meeting well. Elizabeth was a strong swimmer, and it was the one sporting activity at which Owen excelled.

I saw them reach the rock together and heard the tinkle of Elizabeth's laugh before I heard her call 'Go', giving herself several metres start before Owen raced her back to shore.

'Keep watch on our things, Charles,' Elizabeth called. 'Come on, Owen,' and they headed for a grove of cabbage tree palms next to nearby bush.

Owen was no longer in need of my consent. He seemed deliriously happy. His feelings for Elizabeth were transparent. But how did she feel? She certainly seemed to be fond of him. As I sat by myself, not in the least concerned at being excluded, I resolved to find out as soon as I could.

It was twenty minutes before they returned, smiling and laughing.

I arranged a second trip for the three of us to a local beach followed by an evening at the theatre, and was glad when they began to organise their own activities. I had begun to feel like an interloper or chaperon.

After a month of seeing each other, Elizabeth was invited to meet Owen's parents over dinner. You might say that, not being there, I couldn't report what happened with any fidelity. But I think I can. Sometimes we know the protagonists so well, we can write the script of certain scenarios:

Elizabeth: A beautiful meal, Mrs Mortimer. Would you be willing to give me the recipe for the lamb?

Mrs Mortimer: Very kind of you, Elizabeth. I can see you are a discerning judge. Of course I'll give you the recipe.

Mr Mortimer (joking): You know the way to a woman's heart, Elizabeth. And from what I'm hearing, to my son's heart as well.

Owen: Thanks, Dad, but you didn't have to reveal all my secrets.

Mr Mortimer: If only all secrets were that transparent (laughing). What is it that you do, Elizabeth?'

Elizabeth: Secretarial work at the moment, but my lifelong ambition is to get into publishing. I'm not quite sure how, but if I can just get a foothold somewhere, I can build from there. (Mr and Mrs Mortimer exchange looks). What work do you do, Mr Mortimer?

Mr Mortimer: Funny you should ask, Elizabeth, but I'm in publishing myself.

Elizabeth: No! Really?

The night after the dinner, Owen visited me at home. 'You know how I feel about Elizabeth,' he said. 'I haven't exactly hidden my feelings. Has she said anything to you?' For the first time, Owen wasn't self-conscious in baring his feelings.

'You mean about how she feels?' I replied.

He nodded.

'She hasn't said, but I'm sure she feels very strongly. Very strongly,' I repeated, avoiding the word 'love'.

Owen seemed to consider this for some time, his brow creased behind the shock of black hair, before he nodded slowly.

I wanted to ask him what Elizabeth had said to him of her feelings, but his question had given me the answer and, knowing her plan, I began to feel increasingly uneasy. Of course, if nothing further developed in their relationship, I was hardly at fault. I had arranged their coming together, but couldn't be responsible for it lasting. That was what I tried to tell myself, yet I couldn't quite believe it. I knew of Elizabeth's plan, and in a sense I'd promoted it. I'd kept quiet. I was a confederate.

*

'You'll never guess,' an animated Elizabeth said, breezing through the door of my room. 'I start on Monday. Collins.'

I think I succeeded in disguising uneasiness with pleasure at her success. She proceeded to relate the conversation with the Mortimers three days before. It was just as I expected.

'You should have been there, Charles,' she enthused. 'It went like clockwork. And only an hour ago, Pru someone, Mortimer's secretary, rang and offered me a position. Of course I start at the bottom, but I'll work my way up.'

After congratulating her, and sharing in her pleasure, I asked what had been troubling me, trying to sound as casual as possible. 'What's this mean for Owen, sis?'

But Elizabeth was revelling in the flush of success, and a deep and meaningful about her love life was the furthest thing from her mind. She waved the question away.

She'd been with Collins for a month and loving the work when Owen knocked on my door. He was distraught, unshaven, his eyes were bloodshot, and his shirt was hanging out, making him appear more dishevelled than normal.

'Owen, whatever's the matter?' I asked, ushering him to a lounge chair, though I had every reason to suspect the cause of his distress.

'Elizabeth,' he said. 'I saw her with another man.'

'She has lots of friends,' I replied, 'male and female,' realising how facile that might sound.

He must have seen enough to suspect an unwelcome truth.

As he sat slumped in the chair and I planned my next, and hopefully more consoling, strategy, Elizabeth strode into the room, and stopped in her tracks when she saw Owen.

'Owen, what a nice surprise,' sounded trite, as Elizabeth, only for a moment, battled for self-possession.

'No, stay,' Owen said firmly, taking my arm as I started to leave them to confront their problem alone.

Elizabeth remained standing.

'I thought we had something special,' he addressed Elizabeth, who was now behaving as if taken aback by Owen's outburst.

'I thought so too,' Elizabeth held her ground.

'Then why the other man?' Owen said accusingly.

'Owen,' Elizabeth retaliated like a schoolteacher dressing down a student, 'you and I are good friends, we've had good times together, but I've never led you to believe we were anything more than friends.'

Suddenly the room was heavy with silence. Elizabeth felt no need to add anything further. That would be protesting too much. If Owen could have challenged what she said, he probably felt the futility of doing so. For me, there was no way forward. Mediation was out of the question, though I couldn't help wonder if Elizabeth had given Owen reasonable cause to expect more. I suspect she had.

After several minutes of uncomfortable impasse, and near-suffocating silence, Owen was the first to speak.

'I know what you've done, Elizabeth. Suddenly it's all so clear. You knew what I felt for you. I told you often enough. And you certainly led me to believe that you felt the same. It's hard to believe that anyone could be so cruel.'

Elizabeth blanched but had nothing to say as Owen got to his feet and hurriedly left the room without looking at either of us. She followed a minute later, avoiding my eyes and not saying a word.

We didn't see him again. After allowing for a cooling-off period of a couple of days, we both went to see him independently. His flat was deserted and a new tenant was already moving in. He hadn't left a forwarding address. The staff at the Institute of Dramatic Art said he hadn't attended, and had not contacted them.

Elizabeth visited his parents, showing great distress, whether real or assumed. She may have realised that her feelings were stronger than she'd thought. Or she may have been concerned that if Owen had reported his opinion of her motives to his father, her new job would have been in jeopardy. But his parents didn't know he'd gone missing and were intent on comforting her.

The days became weeks and months, and although I hoped that Owen might contact me, if not Elizabeth, we heard nothing. Neither did his parents.

*

With the passing of the years, Elizabeth married Adrian, a financial adviser, but the marriage was unhappy, childless, and ended in divorce after four years. I married Paula a year after Elizabeth's divorce, worked as a government adviser, and lived a life of relative contentment with two children. Apart from the small reversals that present in a life, the financial concerns, and the health issues, there were no major causes for alarm for either of us.

As Elizabeth predicted, she rose through the ranks of Collins to a position of middle management, and had modest success with her own publishing ventures. She enjoyed the work and was mentored by Mr Mortimer, who would ask her every few months if she'd heard anything from Owen. These occasional and heartfelt enquiries kept a nostalgia alive for both of us.

'He was your best mate,' Elizabeth asked me more than once. 'What do you think has happened to him?'

I found myself incapable of predicting.

'Do you think he's still alive?' was a recurring question, and she made frequent references to the good times we'd had, and our having treated him badly.

'I wonder if he still thinks I'm a terrible person,' she said, but only once.

If it was guilt she was feeling, it had been a long time incubating.

Elizabeth had numerous relationships with men. They never seemed intense, didn't seem to bring her more than fleeting satisfaction, and were always short-lived. I still nursed an image of her emerging from the cabbage tree palms at Wattamolla, smiling and laughing, and running with Owen hand in hand into the ocean. It all seemed so different now. She never remarried, and despite the thickening of the body that often comes with middle age, she was still attractive in her early fifties.

I tried a few times to fathom why she lurched from one relationship to another, and when I was finally able to ask the question, I think too bluntly, she answered dismissively, 'A woman has her needs too, you know.'

At about this time, she changed, and I wasn't sure why. I wondered if it had something to do with the sudden death of Mrs Mortimer, with whom she had formed an attachment. She seemed to withdraw from life, though her relationships with men became more frequent and more short-lived. She became increasingly depressed and often looked ill.

'Whatever's the matter?' I asked her. 'I've never seen you so unhappy.'

'Have you heard from Owen?' she asked.

'Elizabeth, if I'd heard from Owen after thirty years, don't you think you'd be the first to know?'

'I want you to find him for me, Charles,' she said abruptly. 'Bring him to me.'

I didn't know what to say. Why did she think I could find him after all this time? Surely his father, with more resources at his disposal than me, must have tried over the years. I'm not sure why, but I thought it was more than likely he was dead. But Elizabeth looked so sick and lacking in her usual spirit, and I was intrigued by this change of heart after thirty years. Or was it a thirty-year-old obsession?

'I'll do everything I can,' I said to appease.

There was little emotion in her reaction.

'You know how difficult it's likely to…' but I stopped when she raised her hand in a brook-no-nonsense gesture.

*

93

Some things are just meant to be. I found him. It may seem hard to believe that after thirty years, and however many attempts by his family to track him down, I should find him when I did. It happened because I attended the funeral of a close friend, and while sitting in the church surrounded by windows where stained-glass shepherds were caught in sections of lead, where an old priest spoke from the pulpit of a life beyond, and people wept, I remembered Owen telling me of Father Hendricks, a priest who'd been an inspiration and mentor. The church had been a trigger.

I had little trouble finding Father Hendricks, now an old and infirm man living in a home with other retired priests, and when I told him an expurgated version of Elizabeth's need, he admitted to being in contact with Owen. The rest was straightforward.

I recognised Owen immediately, even though he looked quite different. The mop of black hair was gone. He was completely bald, his face was heavily lined and weather-beaten, and he walked with a slight stoop. But his brooding eyes didn't lie. I'd learned from Father Hendricks that he'd been married, but wasn't any more, and that two children, now adults, lived in different parts of the world and had little to do with him. I gained the impression that life hadn't been easy.

He'd walked from the station, and sat in the living room of my home, his hands in his lap, making polite conversation interspersed by long silences. I think we both felt estranged from each other.

I'd told him that Elizabeth needed to see him, but she hadn't said why. I wasn't sure myself, and he didn't ask. And it wasn't my business after all these years to pry into his life or ask why he hadn't kept in contact with his parents. Although I told him haltingly a little about myself, he showed no inclination to return the favour.

After a few minutes, I rang Elizabeth, using the family room phone in the hope that hearing my message might create a sense of expectation if not excitement for both of them.

'I'll be there in a sec,' she said breathlessly.

'She's on her way,' I told Owen, hoping it might relieve the tension.

He nodded without apparent emotion.

In only a matter of minutes, the doorbell rang. The three of us were to be together again after all these years. I looked to Owen, and moved to the door.

He stood as I brought Elizabeth into the room.

She stood as if transfixed for a couple of seconds, and gave him a cursory look. 'I don't know this man,' she said. 'Why did you drag me over here?' She was angry, and stormed out of the room.

Owen sat down, outwardly composed.

In the spreading silence, we heard the front door slam, and a car engine start.

*

I walked with Owen to the station, apologising as we walked. I'd brought him all this way for what amounted to another slap in the face.

'There's something else that needs an apology,' I said, and told him of my part in Elizabeth's scheme thirty years before. He listened thoughtfully, but didn't seem surprised, and said he'd always been grateful for my arranging the times for the three of us to meet. I realised from the relief I felt that it must have been playing on my mind for all those years.

I related what I knew of Elizabeth's life and state of mind, the failed marriage, fugitive relationships and depression, as if it might shed some light for him, but he didn't seem overly interested and said nothing.

As we reached the station, I apologised again for luring him away, and said I hoped it wasn't too painful for him. 'It must have been the shock,' I said gently. 'I can't believe that she didn't recognise you,' mindful of not hurting his feelings, but for the first time he actually smiled.

'Yes,' he replied. 'She recognised me all right,' and he paused for a few seconds. 'You can't blame her for wanting to preserve the fantasy. Better the sanctity of memory, than a disappointing reality.'

The light was dimming, it was getting colder, and sutures of light were threading their way across the platform as the train arrived. We shook hands and I never saw him again.

Two Boys

'You know how sometimes we don't know whether to laugh or cry. That's what it was like, Penny. It was hilarious and yet somehow sad. This woman, you've seen her in that marriage reality show on television, came slowly up the red carpet, a real devotee of scenes, but of course with exaggerated composure, all jouncing female parts, insinuating nipples in her strapless bra and her shoehorn-fitted satin gown, and adopts great "what me?" surprise when called for an interview before the cameras that focus on her rather bold décolletage…or is it still décolletage when there are no clothes there?'

Penny began to laugh at Val's burlesque of last night's television coverage of the Academy Awards.

'You wouldn't be exaggerating just a little, Val,' she asked through her laughter. 'Perhaps you should have been nominated for best actor yourself.'

'But Penny, the first however long had nothing to do with films and actors. It was a fashion parade with extra plaudits for the most body-hugging curves and exposed flesh,' Val replied. 'Next year they'll be completely nude.' She was enjoying her own satire.

'And then the host,' Val continued, encouraged by her friend's enjoyment. 'He comes on stage with a swagger to front the world's least funny joke, and with a rare touch of sincerity thanks the industry that fills our ordinary lives with consecrated light. But the worst of it came later when he went from one table to another, followed by the cameras of course, straining to be funny, sitting and chatting with some of the nominees so the television audience could see his blokey touch.'

Penny and Val, both in their early twenties, were flatmates. They'd met again after a couple of years, having been at school together, when Penny went to Val's beauty salon to use a gift voucher she'd been given for a facial. The friendship they'd had at school was quickly re-established.

Theirs was a perfect illustration for those who believe the complementary theory in accounting for friendship. Val, petite and dark, a pocket dynamo, had begun university studies in Arts, but abandoned them when she inherited the salon after her mother's remarriage and move to another state. Penny was tall and blonde, and her natural reserve was a foil for Val's extroversion. She worked as an IT consultant, and did much of her work from home. They'd been flatmates for nine months.

'Well, the not so flattering picture you've just given is the world Jan is hell-bent on entering,' Penny said more soberly.

'Jan who?' Val quipped, smiling.

'OK,' Penny retorted, interpreting the meaning of Val's smile. 'I did hear she'd changed her name. Ocean. Ocean Tremmers.' They were both grinning.

Jan or Ocean lived in the flat next door, and the need for borrowing cups of milk or tea bags, or shopping for each other, made them firm friends, friends in a practical sense, a neighbourly sharing of responsibilities rather than any strong emotional attachment.

Ocean had a swarthy attractiveness and large dark eyes, but was a little buxom for the figure the film and television industry sought. She'd been seduced by the constant admiration of her appearance, and by the applause she'd received in a final year school play, and since leaving school had worked at a number of casual jobs and joined a local amateur theatrical society. She had only just left it, believing that the directors were showing favouritism in not selecting her for a leading role. She had made applications to a few agencies and had been interviewed once, but with no result.

'If I could just be chosen for a television ad, I might get a small part in a series, and then the sky's the limit,' she told Penny and Val one night, daunted by another rejection.

Penny asked her what supporting material or portfolio she presented to the agencies, and Val asked about her appearance and how she dressed when she was promoting herself. They said nothing to her at the time, but later agreed she could do considerably more to enhance her chances.

'What do you think, Penny?' Val asked.

They were both thinking the same thing. Val could give Ocean a makeover in her beauty salon, and help her select the clothes to complement her new looks. Penny could develop an impressive entry on the web, not only saying what the industry would most like to hear, but displaying pictures of Val's handiwork.

'I share your concerns, Val, about the shallowness of the industry,' Penny commented. 'Do you think it's something we should be encouraging? We might be preparing her for an even bigger fall.'

'We're probably being too judgemental,' Val said. 'I'm sure they're not all superficial. Most of them are probably just like you and me. It's just a culture we don't really understand. And it is her passion after all. It's what she lives and breathes.'

'Your name will soon be in lights, Ocean Tremmers.' Penny had the last word, and they both laughed before settling down to discuss a way forward.

*

Ocean was quick to recognise the expertise being offered, particularly when the details were explained, and accepted the offer readily.

'Next week we'll start,' Val said purposefully.

'Sooner if you can,' Ocean, excited by the prospect, answered, embarrassed by her sudden presumption.

Ocean spent several days in Val's salon, experimenting with make-up and hair colouring, streaking, styling and extensions before they settled on a coppery brown with matching extensions. She was given a facial peel, and injectibles to remove wrinkles and give her skin a glow. Val also helped her to choose a couple of complementary outfits and a dieting regime.

Penny started on developing a profile on the web that highlighted, even exaggerated, Ocean's talents, and once Val had finished with the beauty treatments, was able to include alluring photographs. 'Now we wait,' she said.

Within a week, Ocean was called by an agency for an interview, and the result wasn't quite what Penny and Val had expected.

'Guess what.' Ocean came charging into their flat, her eyes alive with excitement. 'I've got an offer. You'll never guess,' she said breathlessly. 'I'm going to be a contestant in a new reality dating show.'

'Is that what you wanted?' Penny asked, trying to conceal disappointment that the offer wasn't a serious acting role.

'They say it'll be watched by tens of thousands.' Ocean's enthusiasm was undiminished. 'It's a start. It's guaranteed exposure. I know it's going to be a big hit.'

And it was. Ocean was a favourite with viewers, playing the coquette, enticing two of the male contestants in the dating game to come to blows, and polarising public opinion. She was either the girl next door, or the tart. She was everything the show's creators wanted.

A one-hour mash-up of the show was also televised, an opportunity to reveal more of the contestants' lives and aspirations. The young television audience was thirsty for more. Extra insight into the contestants' lives was at a premium, as was scandal.

'What advice would you give young people wanting to get started with a career in television?' the interviewer asked Ocean.

'Get yourself a really good portfolio and promote yourself on the web,' Ocean answered, full of self-importance. 'Your appearance and how you present are very important.'

The camera, as if cued, focused on Ocean's face.

'Brains as well as beauty, eh,' the interviewer commented.

'I suppose I'm fortunate to be so blessed,' Ocean said, conscious of the close-up, and striving to appear self-effacing.

'What!' Penny and Val exploded together in their living room. They had been following Ocean in the show, laughing and cringing as the dating scenarios unfolded.

'We don't have to be named,' Penny said, echoing Val's sentiments, 'although it would be nice, but to take the credit for things she knew nothing about…'

'I've been giving her free treatments in the salon.' Val was hurt. 'And do you know, ever since that first week, there's never been a word of thanks.'

'But that's how it is,' Harry shrugged when Penny and Val told him of their grievance. 'That's how their world works.' Harry, now in his seventies, lived alone in the same block of flats. The girls often invited him to dinner, and in return, Harry was a sober voice and good listener, giving wise counsel. He'd come from somewhere in Eastern Europe, where he'd worked behind the scenes in the film industry, and had been retired for many years. 'In one sense,' Harry continued, 'people everywhere are like that, putting themselves first, taking the credit, stealing another's thunder. And in television and film, people get an even more exalted opinion of themselves. It all becomes exaggerated.'

'But don't you think that was mean?' Val queried. 'All she had to do was say she'd had some help.'

'Yes,' Harry answered uncertainly. 'It's all too easy for them to lose sight of what's real. It's a different culture. Talk to her about it, by all means, but I suggest you treat her with kid gloves.'

*

Val needed comforting when she returned home from having spoken to Ocean at the salon about paying for her beauty treatment. 'No, she wasn't exactly upset,' she told Penny. 'A bit sullen, though. I'm sure she expected me to go on doing it for free. Am I being unreasonable?'

'I think you're a saint for having done it for so long,' Penny reassured her.

'Well, she's not exactly a charity case, is she? She's probably earning more than either of us.'

'Quick,' Penny brightened. 'It's her ad again.' She recognised the sound coming from the television in the living room, and Penny knew that the sight of Ocean telling the viewing world with motherly concern and a hint of humour that their backsides would love the softness of Absorbent, the new toilet tissue, was just the therapy Val needed.

It was Ocean's second ad. The first was for Canine Crackers dog food, and showed a dog-loving Ocean rewarding her obedient groodle with a cracker as it sat on the lounge watching television.

She was also given a small part in one of the *Underbelly* series, playing a prostitute trying to seduce a crime boss in a bar. Her entire exposure was only eight to ten seconds, so, in the public eye, she remained 'the dog food lady'.

Even though Ocean continued living next door, there was rarely any contact with her since her moderate success. She didn't seem to come home much, and there were no visitors.

They did see her at a restaurant one Friday night. It was Val's birthday, and already there was an understanding that the two girls would take each other out on their birthdays.

As they were ushered to their table, they saw Ocean sitting with two men and another woman. Ocean saw them too, and quickly looked away, but her dodge didn't go unnoticed by either Penny or Val.

'I think we should at least be gracious,' Val said, 'and say hello.'

Their crossing to the table stilled the raucous laughter, and the four looked up in anticipation. It was obvious that Ocean was not pleased by the intrusion.

'Hello,' Val said cheerily. 'We live next door to Ocean. Couldn't just sit over there and not say hello.'

'Why don't you join us,' one of the men said. 'It's a table for six. You can give us all the low-down on Ocean here,' and he smiled conspiratorially.

'No, no,' Ocean was quick to intercept any answer. 'I'm sure they'd like to be by themselves this evening,' and she gave them a warning look.

The man looked embarrassed. The other gave a shrug. The woman was intrigued.

'He was the man on that news program,' Penny said as they self-consciously made their way back to their table. 'She might have had the courtesy to introduce us.'

*

She was never much of a one for cooking or cleaning, and other domestic chores, even less so since her moderate success. But the accident could have happened to anyone. The oil she was heating in a frying pan ignited, and in her panic, rather than place a lid on the pan to suffocate the flames, she tried to carry it to the sink. Burning oil splashed onto her arms and face.

Penny and Val were home, heard the screams, ran to her flat and comforted Ocean until the ambulance arrived. They followed her to the hospital, the first of several trips they would make in the next ten days.

Ocean needed a skin graft on one arm and plastic surgery on her face. The latter, she was told, would have to wait until the burns 'settled down'.

She didn't seem to be particularly pleased to see Val and Penny, who were later told by the nurses that, apart from them, there had been only one other visitor, a gentleman. It seemed that the industry, having wooed her to serve their own interests, were no longer interested, now that she couldn't deliver what they wanted.

This lack of interest was confirmed when Penny, rushing along George Street, chanced upon the man who'd invited her and Val to sit at Ocean's table at the restaurant.

'You mean to say,' Penny asked, 'that none of her television or film friends have been to see her since the accident?'

'I've been,' the man said defensively, then after a pause, 'I know what you're thinking,' he mellowed, adding, 'and of course you're right. It's a very fickle industry.'

'Will she be able to work again?' Penny asked.

'It depends on how she recovers,' the man answered and shrugged. 'It's a case of being in the right place at the right time.' 'Recovery' of course meant whether she reclaimed her good looks.

'Sometimes something tragic, if you could call her mishap tragic, has a way of bringing us to our senses,' Val commented, having heard Penny's recount of what the man had said.

'You think she might now realise what real friendship means?' Penny added.

'I remember in my early teenage years,' Val confided, 'I was horrible to my mother. I was a real little bitch. Not doing what she asked, answering back, pinching her jewellery without asking. And then I got really sick. Of course Mum was always there, making silent sacrifices the way mums do. It was a lesson for me. I've never been mean to her since, not deliberately anyway.'

'Let's hope it's the same for Ocean,' Penny said gently, rubbing Val's shoulder to show her concern.

Ocean was sullen when she returned home from hospital. She had reluctantly given Penny and Val the key to her flat, and they had cleaned it, bought fresh flowers for the bedroom and living room, and had prepared three casseroles. Ocean was still waiting for her plastic surgery, and her cheek and forehead on one side of her face were disfigured. She was obviously depressed, and would lie in bed during the day for hours at a time, occasionally getting up to play the tapes of her ads and performance in *Underbelly*.

Penny and Val came separately and often together to see her, trying to lighten her mood, but she had little to say to them. The more cheerful they were, the more Ocean seemed to resent it.

'I know what you're trying to do,' she said to them one evening. 'It's all very well for you two, look at you, good jobs, pretty…'

'But Ocean,' Penny interrupted, 'after the plastic surgery, you'll be back to your beautiful self.'

'Oh sure,' Ocean replied aggressively. 'We all know it's the end for me. Just go, both of you! I don't need your help, and I certainly don't need your sympathy.'

Penny and Val left, indignant and hurt, and after a few minutes at home sharing their resentment, went straight to Harry.

'I can tell where you've been,' he said as he opened the door. 'It's written all over your faces.'

'She was really mean, Harry,' Val answered sitting down woodenly. 'Again!'

Penny added, 'Yet again!' joining her on the lounge. 'That's it as far as I'm concerned. No point reaching out any more to get knocked down.'

'Excuse us for caring,' Val said with heavy irony.

Anticipating their need, Harry made drinks for them all, and sat opposite, sipping his wine and deep in thought. Penny and Val knew the familiar look, a prelude to revelation.

'Let me tell you a story about two boys I knew growing up in the old country where I came from. Vlado and Laszlo were the best of friends. They lived next door to each other, were in the same class at school, they had the same interests, and they defended each other against bullies. Entering their teenage years didn't change the strength of their friendship, though Laszlo was also devoted to a girl called Cindy.

'They were both excellent swimmers. Laszlo was the stronger of the two, but not by much. As eighteen-year-olds, they competed against each other to determine who would represent their district at the national championships. They were the two strongest swimmers in the race so, short of some big surprise, it was really between the two of them. Winning was very important to Vlado, and when he won the race, he knew that Laszlo had let him touch the wall first. But he didn't let on that he knew. Laszlo was pleased for him, congratulated him, bought him new goggles as a present, and helped him in his training.

'Vlado went on to win the nationals, and in his speech at a

celebratory dinner in his home town, with all sorts of dignitaries present, he thanked everyone who'd helped him along the way, even the pool attendant, everyone except Laszlo, who was deeply hurt. But that wasn't the end of it.'

Penny and Val were sitting forward on the lounge, willing him to continue.

'What do you young ones say now? Vlado "made a move" on Laszlo's girl. He even went so far as telling some untruths about Laszlo. And Cindy, the girl, seduced by Vlado's newly won status, left Laszlo and started to go out with him instead. Their friendship was over. But why did Vlado do it?'

Penny and Val were watching Harry questioningly, not daring to interrupt.

'Was he punishing Laszlo for the goodness he could never repay? Did he feel guilty about omitting Laszlo from his list of thankyous, and decide to cover his tracks by all-out attack rather than being defensive?' Harry paused for a moment.

Penny and Val were silent.

Harry stroked his chin then, picking up the thread, 'Some great writer said 'that the hardest thing for rational man to do is to apologise. Perhaps when you start being cruel to someone, it's hard to reverse the process.'

'What happened to them?' Val asked after half a minute's further silence.

'I don't know what happened to Laszlo,' Harry replied in a whisper, 'but Ocean isn't the only one who can change names.'

*

Ocean's plastic surgery was miraculous. After three months there was barely a mark on her face, certainly none that make-up couldn't disguise. Penny and Val saw little of her in that time, and assumed that she had been welcomed back by the industry that had deserted her in her time of need.

But it soon became apparent that Ocean was spending most of the days at home, and Harry suggested a possible reason.

'Four months can be an eternity in the television and film industry,' he said. 'In all likelihood, things have moved on. Ocean might not be what they're looking for any more.'

Harry's speculation gave the girls food for thought.

'Have you ever thought any more of Harry's story, the one about the two boys?' Penny asked Val.

'Strange you should mention it, but yes, I have. A lot,' Val replied. 'Especially lately.'

They had not discussed its significance, and had not referred to it since Harry told it.

'Should we?' Penny offered tentatively, looking pointedly at Val, and knowing that she understood the meaning of her unfinished question.

That same night, they knocked on the door of Ocean's flat for the first time in three months. She greeted them uncertainly, but they entered the room and sat down. Ocean waited uneasily for them to speak.

'You can tell us to mind our own business,' Penny began gently, 'but if you think it might be a good thing to reinvent yourself, give yourself a new image, Val and I would like to help…do what we did before, only better…I could do a new web page, write about your journey, highlight what you've achieved.'

'And I have some ideas about a fresh appearance,' Val added, not wanting to seem too enthusiastic in case Ocean took offence and saw it as implied criticism.

They saw the light emerging in Ocean's wide-open eyes, and the rapid nodding of her head in the expectant silence of the room. But with their departure, they didn't see her rush to her bedroom, throw herself on the bed, and start sobbing.

A Two-sided Story

As a single man in my mid-thirties, a reluctantly uncommitted bachelor, I had learned over many lonely years to initially accept and eventually value my independence. Living by yourself for too long makes you selfish, jealous of your freedom, and increasingly unable to negotiate a shared life. At least that's the commonly held view. So when the doorbell rang at eleven one Friday night, I wasn't particularly happy. And at that late hour there was cause for alarm.

'Can I come in, James?' Trudi stood at the door in the wan porch light clutching a small cloth handbag. Even in jeans and sweatshirt she looked dishevelled, and her cheeks were carbon-streaked where tears had made her mascara run.

'I'm not going to say no,' I said, instantly realising that I may have sounded flippant. 'Of course, of course,' I added quickly, and seeing her distress, I put my arm around her shoulders as we moved to the lounge room. 'Whatever's the matter?' I asked gently as we hugged, and her tears began to flow again.

'It's Myles,' she said. 'He hit me.'

We sat down together on the lounge. Myles was her husband and my long-standing best friend, so I was anxious to hear her story, and curious as to why she'd chosen me.

'You'd better tell me what happened,' I said, taking her hand.

But Trudi didn't need my invitation to launch into her grievance. 'We were talking about nothing in particular, I can't even remember what. It all became heated, and he started to shout. Then he hit me. Whack! Here!' and she turned to show me the other side of her face that was distinctly red and swollen in the brighter lounge room light.

I was taken aback. It wasn't like Myles at all. I'd known him since our kindergarten days, and in all that time, I'd never seen him riled. But I was wary of asking Trudi if she had said anything to provoke him. That might have been provocative on my part.

'He must have been very frustrated,' I said instead. 'It's not the Myles I know.'

'He's not the placid man you think he is, James.' There was steel in her voice. 'He's threatened me before.'

I asked the usual questions about his state of mind, pressures at work, financial worries, concern for his terminally ill mother, health issues of his own that he might have kept from us both.

'Did you come straight here?' I asked, curious about the time, and wondering if their altercation had only just happened.

'I've been with Esme,' she answered, 'and she thinks I should go to the police.'

Esme was her close friend, whose husband had left for a younger woman years before, and who I reckoned disliked men in general.

'I think that's a little premature,' I said hastily, mindful of the remorse Myles was probably feeling. 'Let me talk to him, Trudi. Perhaps I can get to the bottom of it.'

What bottom of it, I thought as I said it. The why? Some deeper underlying reason? A predisposition of Myles I knew nothing about?

Trudi seemed to consider this before she reluctantly agreed, but warned that she would not stand for it being 'swept under the carpet'. 'Do you think it's safe to go home?' she asked.

I could understand her anxiety, yet I felt a little irritated. Perhaps I considered it an over-reaction. Did she really think he would be waiting, determined to inflict more harm?

'I'm sure it is,' I answered. 'He's probably worried out of his mind.'

She offered a smeared cheek to be kissed and clung to me for a long time at the unopened front door. There was a faint smell of eau de cologne with the saltiness of tears. She left without another word.

*

I've often found that close male friends baulk at direct confrontation, preferring to sidle up to it. Trudi had told Myles of her visit to me, so he was expecting my call. We met in a coffee shop we visited together at least once a month. The adage of there being two sides to every story, at least when there are only two protagonists, was uppermost in my mind, but one side became considerably less defensible if violence were involved.

'How are the two of you getting on?' I began. I couldn't have been less direct, but Myles understood.

'I did hit her,' he answered my disguised question. 'I know I shouldn't have,' he continued without embarrassment. 'You know how we're told, James, that you never hit a woman, not under any circumstances. Well, I'm not so sure I agree. If a child is naughty, you might give it a warning tap on the backside. If people are hysterical, you do what you must to subdue them. But what if an adult is violent in every non-physical way, cruel, out of control…then an arresting slap may be the answer,' and he quickly added, 'as long as that's all it is.'

The words came with such vehemence, it was obvious that Myles had been mulling over what happened. Rationalising perhaps?

'I'm not sure I agree,' I said, but it wasn't the time or place to pursue the argument. 'Is that all it was, mate?' The 'mate' jarred, smacked of football and pubs. I'd never called him that before. It was meant to flag our special friendship. 'A slap, a single slap…open hand?'

'Yes,' Myles seemed surprised. 'Why? What did she tell you?' He looked at me with alarm.

'Nothing different.' I was quick to retreat.

We sipped our coffee and ate our raisin toast without talking for a couple of minutes. People came and left in quick succession, eager for their morning fix. An old couple at the next table hadn't said a word, but stared beyond each other, their minds seemingly empty as fallow fields.

'Look, James,' Myles resumed, 'things aren't good between us. That'll hardly surprise you. They haven't been good for a long time now. But in the last four to six months…'

And Myles related a catalogue of Trudi's verbal abuse. She was scornful of his failure to be promoted at work; she belittled his efforts at undertaking electrical and plumbing repairs in the house; she criticised his eating, his driving, his appearance; and what she called 'his countless infuriating mannerisms'. But it wasn't the usual light-hearted ribbing between partners. What he found most hurtful was the venom with which she did so. At least that was Myles's story.

'It isn't just a case of innocently pressing the wrong buttons,' he explained. 'I'm beginning to think,' he concluded, 'that she's trying damn hard to provoke me, to get me to do something I'll regret.'

'If that's the case,' I counselled, 'refuse to be drawn, don't react at all. Button your lips. Just smile sweetly.'

And we both gave each other a saccharine smile, and laughed. But I still felt uneasy. Trudi would be anxious to quiz me on the outcome of our talk. What could I tell her?

*

Trudi was my girlfriend before she met Myles, though claiming her as mine suggests some possession, and I'm not sure that was the case. She belonged to everyone, and no one.

She lived one street away, so it was easy as maturing adolescents to go swimming together at the nearby beach. We attended school dances together, and while we went in different directions after leaving school, we'd occasionally accompany each other to the theatre. There was no one special in her life. I'd have known if there was.

Attempting to further our friendship beyond one of convenience, I bought her a sterling silver bracelet from an antique jewellery store. I think it was Indian or Turkish, with intricate etching, and very expensive. Tormented by whether or not it was appropriate to have it engraved, I eventually had my initials 'JW' inscribed on the underside, so it would only be visible to her when she removed it, a suitably subtle concession to sentiment. She loved it and wore it everywhere. But it didn't change the nature of our relationship.

I introduced her to Myles, and before they became more serious about each other, we did a lot together as part of a large group. She was always animated. Some called her 'out there' or 'larger than life'. I can still see the look on her face after her success at rock climbing. We'd all been to a rock-climbing venue when the sport had gained in popularity and indoor places had begun to appear. A few of the men and most of the women found the climbing difficult, either from lack of coordination, lack of strength, or fear.

'Look at me! Watch this!' Trudi called to us as we were idly chatting on the ground, and when she had gained our attention, she scaled the vertical rock face to the top, swivelled around in her harness and shouted 'Da da,' raising her hand in salute and scanning our faces with delight.

I saw less of her as her relationship with Myles grew. They obviously wanted time alone, and I contented myself with other members of the group, most of whom were single. Sometimes the original members of the group reunited when there was a funeral, wedding, graduation or special performance.

One such occasion was Trudi's starring role in an amateur production of a Noel Coward comedy at the local theatre. A number of us had been approached, even coerced, into listening to her rehearse her lines and read the 'other' part to 'lead her in', while she played the prima donna, both the part the play demanded, and the part that wasn't demanded by us harangued non-thespians.

She was a great success on the night, revelling in the congratulations we all gave her, continuing in character for hours after the play had finished, and asking me on a couple of occasions since, 'Was I all right, James?'

I was best man at their wedding three years ago, a glittering occasion at which Trudi broke with the convention of all-male speeches, and spoke herself. They honeymooned in Fiji, and I thought myself fortunate to receive a card they'd both written.

I assumed both she and Myles were happy. I can't recall any

incident that would make me think otherwise. Perhaps we too readily accept the general belief that marriage is a threshold, an arrival of sorts, and a leaving behind of old scores. Even an automatic conferral of contentment.

After they'd settled down in a house a few streets from my own, and not far from where they'd both lived before, Myles and I resumed our monthly meetings for coffee, alter egos swapping stories of remembered follies, not that there were many, and what might have been.

*

It happened again. This time Trudi said she was pushed and had fallen, hitting her arm on the leg of a table. She'd left the house and gone straight to Esme's, and they'd gone to the police station together.

Despite Esme's grandstanding, a male and a female officer treated the accusation seriously. A number of deaths from domestic violence had recently occurred, and no officer wanted to be red-faced when warning signs had been ignored.

Myles suffered the indignity of being visited at home by the two police officers, while Trudi stayed with Esme. He was grilled on his version of the event, and asked if there'd been any history of physical abuse. Knowing that Trudi had been to the police station, he wasn't going to fall for the trap, and admitted to the earlier slap. Both officers appeared grim-faced when he did so.

'You're not normally an aggressive person,' the older female officer said. 'Several of your friends say you're docile, in fact.'

To add to Myles's humiliation, Trudi had given them the names of some of our friends who had been readily contacted. At that stage, Trudi hadn't consulted me. Perhaps she was disappointed that my efforts hadn't 'got to the bottom of it' after all. Or it was more likely that she suspected I owed my greater loyalty to Myles.

'We see this every day,' the female officer continued. 'Some of the men you see on the news aren't unlike yourself. They're not monsters. But these things have a way of escalating, and our job is to make sure that doesn't happen.'

'She hasn't pressed charges.' The male officer seemed to have some sympathy. 'But if it happens again, we'll have to take more serious action.'

'Meanwhile,' the female officer took up the thread, 'here's the name of someone we want you to see, someone who might be able to help,' and she handed Myles a calling card. 'I'm sorry, but it's not negotiable. We'll be checking to see that you've been.'

'What on earth…' I began when I met Myles the following day. He was grey and haggard, and didn't look at all well. I could see it was no longer the time for confrontation, even between close friends, so we waited in silence for our coffee, before he began.

He explained that she had been goading him, telling him he was a hopeless lover, and that some of our other male friends were a far better sexual prospect than him.

'I've a mind to find out,' she'd told him. 'Now, who first…Brad or Jesse?'

I was grateful that my name wasn't included.

'She got into real intimate stuff,' Myles whispered. 'Threw it in my face.'

He hadn't touched his coffee.

'I went to leave the room…actually thought of your advice…but she reached the door first and barred the way. I gave her a gentle push…look, like this,' and he motioned me to stand, intent on a demonstration, and pushed me so that I took a step backwards but easily maintained my balance.

A few of the coffee shop customers looked at us curiously.

'James, it sounds incredible, but I think she deliberately threw herself backwards. It was so clumsy…ham acting.'

I tried to reassure Myles, though I could see no way forward. 'I'm not saying you have a problem, Myles, but I think it's important you see this counsellor,' I said. 'And the sooner the better. You don't have a choice anyway.'

I was disturbed when we parted. Myles admitted to two incidents that, while arguably minor, could certainly be called assault. Extreme provocation, even if true, might be a mitigating factor, but not an excuse. What was the real story? I'd never had reason to disbelieve Myles before, but we do construct our own realities to suit ourselves. Was it a case of the accused saying, 'Your honour, he kept banging his head against my fists?'

Trudi of course gave me a different version. If she had been provocative, it was nothing out of the ordinary. I thought it best not to ask her about the alleged nature of her provocation. Myles had been unnecessarily violent. She held me again, saying what an ordeal it had all been, and how grateful she was to have a friend like me.

*

I was with Myles when the same two police officers arrived. Trudi hadn't returned home from Esme's; at least that is what I was led to believe.

Myles looked disturbed as he answered the door. 'What is it this time?' he asked ungraciously.

'I think you know very well what it's about, Mr Tanner,' the male officer replied testily. The formality didn't augur well.

I looked at Myles, and he returned my look with a blank stare, and a shrug.

'What did she say he's done, officer?' I tried to ease the tension.

'She didn't have to say anything,' the female officer replied. 'She's in the hospital with a couple of broken ribs and heavy bruising. But don't you worry, Mr Tanner, we'll be getting the full story tomorrow when she's up to talking.'

I looked inquiringly at Myles again, but he avoided my look, choosing to stare out the window instead. Broken ribs and deep bruising were more serious than a reddened face and a shove causing a fall. Myles had admitted to the previous two, but how could he possibly explain this? What was the provocation this time?

'Mr Tanner, we did tell you that these things can escalate very quickly, and you haven't seen the contact we gave you. You haven't even made an appointment.'

'I hadn't forgotten,' Myles said absent-mindedly. 'I was getting round to it.'

The two officers looked at each other and shook their heads.

'I'm afraid you'll be coming with us, Mr Tanner,' the male officer warned. 'Come along now.'

They had treated Myles fairly, and at least allowed him to walk by himself to the car without restraint.

*

I visited Trudi the following day in the hospital. It's what Myles would have wanted. Her midriff was heavily bandaged, and the bruises on her arms were black and yellowy green. She kissed me fondly and asked me to sit close to her at the head of the bed. The police had already been and taken a statement.

I waited for her to explain what had happened, as she had done before, but she continued to talk perfunctorily about the weather, hospital food, and a few of our common friends.

'What did you tell the police?' I asked, taking her hand.

'What's to tell?' she replied. 'I mean, look at me, James. How do you think this happened? I didn't just wake up with it.'

I wondered if her reluctance to give me the details was because she knew that if I'd already spoken to Myles, he would certainly have given me a different version that might cast doubt on her own. I didn't think I'd let on to either of them that I believed one over the other.

'Did you tell the police the full story, Trudi?' I was trying to understand just how serious the problem was for Myles.

Trudi suddenly looked very angry, reached for the alarm bell and began to shout for help. Two nurses came running, and a male visitor in the same ward hurried over. I was taken by surprise and unable to react for a few moments.

'Trudi, whatever's the matter?' I whispered, trying to soothe her.

She had already pulled her hand free of mine.

'Is he upsetting you, miss?' the male visitor asked, looking at me threateningly.

'I want him out of here,' Trudi pleaded with the two nurses. 'Get him out! Please!'

'I'll have to ask you to leave, sir,' the younger nurse said.

'If you don't leave this instant,' the other ordered, 'I'll have security escort you, and they might not be gentle about it.'

Trudi was already clinging to the young nurse, her arms around her neck, even though she was wincing with pain.

The three of them stood guard by the bedside as I left without a backward look.

*

By late the following day, Myles was still at the police station and hadn't been charged. But it was only a matter of time. I'd been allowed one phone call, but his talk was closely monitored and, apart from the expected reaction of resignedly declaring his innocence, I'd learned nothing more. I'd resolved that it would be a long time before I graced Trudi with my presence again.

When the doorbell sounded at five-thirty p.m., I assumed it was something to do with Myles. Probably the police, or concerned friends. It wasn't.

She introduced herself as Mrs Hargreaves, a stout woman of sixtyish in a plaid skirt, and a salmon-pink pullover. She had a kind grandmotherly face. 'You don't know me, Mr Williams,' she began, 'but I have a little surprise for you,' and she reached into her handbag and pulled out the silver bracelet I'd given Trudi years ago.

'I rather fancy myself as Miss Marple,' she said and laughed, 'but I looked at the initials JW on the underside, and because it looked so expensive, I took it to that antique jewellers in Cooper Street, and asked if it came from there, and if they kept a record of sale. And bingo! Here I am.' Mrs Hargreaves was delighting in her cleverness.

'It's a beautiful piece. I'm sure the lovely lady in your life will be very relieved,' she beamed, 'and I do so hope that she will be better soon.'

'I beg your pardon,' I said, nonplussed.

'The accident,' she replied, looking at me curiously, 'when she fell onto the rocks at the beach. I'm afraid I was too far away to help straight away, and she seemed to be in so much pain, but she had somehow managed to drive away before I arrived. My poor old legs aren't what they used to be. But her bracelet was there. Poor soul,' she added, 'and not even a single person there to lend a helping hand.'

A Leopard's Spots

Miss Dodd did have another name: Eunice. But she made it very clear to everyone that she preferred they not use her Christian name, if they were lucky enough to discover what it was, and that to do so would be overfamiliar. 'Miss Dodd is quite adequate,' she would tell those who asked.

White-haired, tiny and slightly stooped, with penetrating blue eyes, she had lived in the same very large house in one of the better addresses for over eighty years. Her two older sisters had married well, she liked to say by way of explanation, over sixty years ago and, with the death of their parents, were generous enough to sign the property over to her. They too were both gone now.

It was a double-storey brick house with five large bedrooms and two bathrooms on a flat quarter-acre block. It had many old-world touches like elaborate cornices and carved oak banisters on the staircase but, still boasting its original decor, it was tired. The carpets were worn, walls needed painting or repapering, and the bathrooms still retained their original tiles and silver taps that had started to drip years ago.

'I don't think I can go on rattling around in here for much longer,' she told Mark. 'It's getting to the time for me to move on, for someone to look after me.'

'Nonsense, Miss Dodd.' Mark pooh-poohed the idea. 'You're still mobile, you still have your wits about you, and besides, you know you can call on me to do all the things that need to be done.'

'You're too kind, my dear,' she said affectionately, 'but I need a stick now just to get around the house, a walking frame for outside, and as for my wits as you call them, I can't remember where I've put anything, and only this morning I forgot the name of that nice woman next door.'

Mark Joplin, a single man in his early thirties, tall, and rugged if not handsome, who lived in the next suburb, had been helping Miss Dodd now for a month, ever since he helped her carry her parcels from the supermarket. He'd driven her home that day, shown a welcome interest in the house, and had undertaken to do some of the more necessary jobs around the place.

He'd found a ladder in the shed, and cut several branches off the jacaranda that was growing over the roof, making a clattering sound above Miss Dodd's bedroom, interrupting her sleep, and depositing its springtime lilac to decay in the gutters. He nailed back a number of palings that had fallen from the side fence, thus preventing the raids of Mr Button's small shrub-destroying dog. He mowed the lawn and cleared the paspalum that was licking the sides of the house.

'I'm very grateful, my dear, for everything you've done for me. You've been too kind.'

'It's been a pleasure to help such a lovely lady,' Mark quipped.

'Are you trying to charm the old girl,' Miss Dodd said with mock dignity, enjoying the badinage.

'You mentioned leaking taps,' Mark replied. 'I've been doing things outside, but there are probably some things I might be able to help you with inside.'

'You go ahead,' she told him, after they'd inspected the downstairs rooms together. She seemed a little inconvenienced, and was leaning heavily on her walking stick. 'I'll sit for a moment.'

Mark walked purposefully up the stairs, and it was an age before he returned. Miss Dodd looked up inquiringly, momentarily confused. She'd been asleep for a minute or two, and her glasses had fallen down her nose.

'I can probably fix the taps,' Mark said, 'if I find the right tools. The mirror's come away from its backing in your bedroom, the Manet print's sitting on the floor, and the bed legs in the second bedroom need to be secured. No problem.'

'Thank you, dear,' she answered. 'You're such a good boy.'

*

'I can't believe anyone could do that,' Beth sobbed. 'I feel such a fool.'

'Put it behind you,' her flatmate Samantha consoled her. 'He's not worth the time of day,' and after she saw the doubtful look on her friend's face, 'You're not going to say you still care? Beth, he's a monster!'

'We were going to settle down together.' Beth was still trying to stretch the elastic of probability. 'He was looking for a place.'

'Did he actually propose?' Samantha asked curtly, impatient from Beth's refusal to accept the inevitable.

'Not in so many words,' Beth answered, 'but he kept talking about our life together.'

In her late thirties, Beth was ruddy-faced, and a little plump, with curly, sandy-coloured hair and hazel eyes. She'd not been married, but had suffered two torturous love affairs with painful endings.

So when Mark showed a keen interest, she regarded it as a last chance, even a form of redemption. He was several years younger, but the difference was not so great that it mattered. Friends and parents were increasingly referring to the ticking of her biological clock, and she was keen to have a family, but not at the expense of love. She'd mentioned it to Mark, teasing his ego with 'It's not too late to have another little Joplin', but he had been evasive.

They'd met at the supermarket, where he'd offered his assistance. She'd been grateful for the help, and began to talk with him in the car park while her tub of ice cream melted. He'd asked for her number, and while she didn't expect to hear from him, she hoped she would. She did.

'I have two tickets,' he said, a by-the-way, offhand invitation that's a little like saying, 'I'd like you to come, but if you can't…'

She was pleased, particularly as it was to a musical that she loved. She would learn later that it wasn't really his scene.

It was a whirlwind romance. He'd bring her flowers and chocolates, and she'd take him back to her flat for the night.

Samantha wasn't impressed by what she considered an intrusion, and didn't warm to Mark. 'There's something, I don't know what, but something I'm not altogether comfortable with,' she told Beth later, much to her friend's annoyance.

His attentions escalated. He declared his love. He bought her gifts. He told her she was the best thing that had ever happened to him.

If only Samantha had known. Despite the cruelties that fate had handed out to Beth, pain that is often potential sophistication, she was surprisingly naïve. She was convinced that life had finally been kind and that Mark was the chosen one. So when he'd suggested, almost casually, that with their future in mind, it might be financially viable to create a joint bank account, and that he could see to it if she agreed, she saw it as a step forward in their relationship. She withdrew her savings from her bank account and gave it to him.

'I can't believe you did that,' an incredulous Samantha had said. 'Whatever were you thinking? How much did you give him?'

'Seventy thousand dollars. Everything. But can't you see,' Beth had appealed, becoming irritated, 'it means that we're one now…facing life together with common responsibilities.'

'I hope you're right,' Samantha said, not believing it for a moment.

When Mark didn't call the Saturday after the transaction, Beth was disappointed but thought nothing of it. People have unexpected work and family commitments that explain such absences.

But it didn't take long for uneasiness to become alarm. He used to call every day. After four or five days, she wondered if Samantha's fears were grounded, but even then guiltily dismissed the thought. There had to be some credible explanation.

Even after their three months of being together, Beth didn't have his address or phone number. He'd told her that he moved around a lot with his work, and was sometimes incommunicado. She had believed him. He had told her, though, that he shopped every couple of days at the supermarket.

A furious Samantha waited there for an hour or two on consecutive days, and was fortunate enough to accost him late one afternoon a week after his last contact with Beth. She asked him what game he was playing.

He looked surprised. 'Game?' he queried. 'If you're referring to Beth,' he said, 'it didn't work out…it was never meant to be.'

'Did you tell her that?' She was incensed. 'And what about her money?'

'What money?' he answered, and hurried away.

*

Mark's 'recruiting' venue was the local supermarket. It was a place where women, mostly alone, shopped for their families or for themselves, and were often weighed down with parcels or harassed by domestic responsibilities. They were usually grateful for offers of help, sometimes willing to talk, and Mark, who could be quite charming, was quick to identify a target. Sometimes it was done for him, like the time he heard two women chatting at the checkout.

'I often see them in here,' one said. 'They seem a loving couple, always holding hands.'

'They're lovely old people,' the other said, 'old-fashioned values, I reckon, but they've known their fair share of tragedy too. Daughter, I seem to remember her name was Allison, early thirties, died of cancer a few years back.'

The lovely old couple was Howard and Audrey Nicholls, both in their early seventies, members of community committees, regular volunteers, contributors to a variety of charities, and comfortable but by no means rich. Apart from Allison, they had a son who lived in another state and had a family of his own.

'May I help you with those,' Mark said ingratiatingly, pointing to their shopping. 'You must be feeding an army.'

'Why, thank you,' Audrey Nicholls replied. 'We only have to wheel the trolley to the car. But it's nice to meet someone so courteous.'

'I hope you don't mind me asking.' Mark had already identified his target. 'But you look remarkably like a girl I knew years ago, name of Allison.'

Howard and Audrey were suddenly interested, and happy to talk to a nice young man, their daughter's age and who might revive pleasant memories of her.

The rest was easier than he first thought. He seemed to remember meeting her through a friend, or it might have been school, asked what school she went to, and in what years, and feigned surprise when they answered. 'That's where it must have been!'

'She passed on four years ago,' Howard said matter-of-factly. They had long since placed her death in the perspective of their lives, seen it as the will of God.

'Oh, I'm so sorry.' Mark displayed apparent distress.

'Look, why don't you come back to the house,' Audrey asked. They were still standing in the car park. 'I have photos of Allison, and I bought a Chelsea bun.'

Mark proved to be a gracious guest. The Nicholls talked at length about Allison, recalled her death from lymphoma, and were astonished to learn that the befriended young man suffered from the same cancer.

'How are you coping? Audrey asked, all concerned, and feeling that here was a kindred spirit of Allison's.

Mark assumed that a show of emotion for this couple was not the way to go. Dignity was called for. He was as composed as possible, reported that his cancer had only just been diagnosed and, although he went to St George Hospital, he couldn't recall the doctor's name. It had been such a shock and the medical, not to mention the financial, implications were yet to be realised.

'No, definitely not,' he said when Howard Nicholls, after a private consultation with Audrey in the kitchen, wrote him a personal cheque for ten thousand dollars. 'I couldn't possibly…' But he did.

It was weeks before the Nichollses discovered the truth. Allison had died at St George Hospital. They were well known to staff, and in contact with some of them, so it was only a matter of time. Their grief returned. They found it hard to believe that someone could be so cruel, and they saw it as a betrayal of Allison. They blamed themselves.

For a few weeks, Mark went either very early or late to the supermarket, thinking it wise to keep a low profile. Besides, he had other fish to fry. In a country town miles away, disguised as best he could, he ran a book on the weekend races, and absconded with the money, owing thousands to the punters. He persuaded another woman to make an investment of three thousand dollars on some gold stocks that in a day or so would go through the roof. Entrusting him with the money to expedite the matter, and beguiled by his charm, she never heard from Mark again. The name of the company was not even listed.

*

For a man of Mark's talent in selecting a target, it's not difficult to see why Miss Dodd was such a prize prospect. She was single with no living relatives, old and doddery both physically and mentally, and not averse to moving into a care facility or possibly even relinquishing some of her wealth before she died.

From Mark's perspective, he had put in the hard yards. He'd spent time doing work both inside and outside the house for a couple of months, only briefly interrupted by his affair with Beth. He considered it important to gain her trust. All the while, he'd been trying to decide on a plan.

'It's been a while, dear,' she commented, pleased to see him, but not getting up from her chair.

'I've been very busy, Miss Dodd.' Mark answered, as if an apology was expected. 'But I had to hurry back to see my favourite person. Do you have things for me to do?'

'Always plenty here for you to do, dear.'

'Have you given any more thought to moving somewhere that people can look after you…leaving this big house?'

Miss Dodd didn't answer directly but proceeded with a litany of ills. She looked paler and smaller as though she'd shrunk. 'I'm finding it harder to do the shopping. My legs won't do what I tell them to do. I had a fall the day before yesterday, got my foot caught in the bed-clothes and down I went, no damage, at least not this time. And I miss getting out in the garden. I'm afraid it's a lost cause.'

A few days later, Mark took Miss Dodd to an age care facility that boasted a fine reputation. There was a garden apartment with a mass of flowers, hanging baskets and two large bedrooms. The apartment was about to be vacated. It faced surrounding bush and was visited daily by crimson rosellas. That won Miss Dodd. Meals were served in a dining room, or in certain cases could be brought to rooms. They had to move quickly. The facility manager agreed to allow them a fortnight's grace to make a holding deposit before the present occupants vacated.

'You'll need a good lawyer, and in a hurry,' Mark said on the way home.

'Oh dear.' Miss Dodd was flustered. 'I don't know how to go about it.'

'I could handle it for you.' Mark could hardly contain his excite-ment. This was what he had been working so hard to achieve. It was all falling into place. 'You'd have to trust me completely of course. There might be people you'd much rather…'

'Oh no, dear. If you could…'

And so Mark arrived several days later with a folder of documents for Miss Dodd to sign. 'It's a deed of sale for your house,' he said. 'You need the money to buy your way into the village. Do you want me to explain how it'll work?'

'I wouldn't understand, dear,' Miss Dodd replied. 'You handle it. I don't know how I'll ever be able to thank you.'

'We both sign. Quite a few pages, I'm afraid. A copy for us both. One for me to give to the solicitor, and the other for you to keep. The places are marked by a cross. I'll give you a minute or two,' and he left for the lavatory in his excitement, leaving Miss Dodd peering through her glasses at the unopened document.

When he returned, she was signing the final page with a laboured signature. He signed the pages speedily, and in his exhilaration gave her a peck on the cheek that startled her before leaving. He turned at the door and saw her, small, pale, almost transparent like a spectre. But it was no time for misgivings.

*

It was the same picture of Miss Dodd he met when he returned ten days later. It wasn't a meeting he relished, though he did think his labours for her had gone unrewarded. All that work, and for what? Still, she wasn't such a bad old stick.

Like so many older people of her generation, she accepted the slings and arrows of fortune without great emotional fuss. 'You mean I can't go to the village home at all?' she asked resignedly.

'I'm afraid not,' Mark answered.

'Then I suppose I'll just have to stay here. I've lived here my whole life. I might as well die here,' she said after a long silence.

'That's not possible either.' Mark was definite. 'You signed your house over to me. It's mine now. But I am willing to give you time to find somewhere else.'

It was only then that the awful truth seemed to dawn on Miss Dodd. She raised her head to fix him with a steely look, her mouth half-open in shocked disbelief. 'But I have nowhere to go. Where will I go and what with?'

'There might be welfare places that will take you.' Mark was not sympathetic.

'You. It was you. You organised the whole thing! You worked at getting my trust, and now this.' Her voice trailed away. She was shaking. What little colour there was had drained from her face.

Mark hurriedly got to his feet and made for the door. He'd given her the ultimatum. It had to be done. Others might think he had done some dastardly things, but he didn't think so. If there was a line that couldn't be crossed, he hadn't come across it yet.

'Why? Why?' he heard her croak as he reached the door.

'Have you heard of Charles Darwin, Miss Dodd?' he answered. 'Survival of the fittest. That's what this world is based on. The strong ones get the rewards, and the weaker ones fall by the wayside. In the end, it's all about one person dominating another, or more powerful groups exercising control over others, and over what the world has to offer. It's about power. The animal kingdom shows no sympathy. A leopard doesn't change its spots. And we're all animals after all.'

With that, he left and didn't look back.

*

Two days later, a much-improved Miss Dodd was entertaining two women, one young and one older in her home. She served tea from her Royal Albert cups, and scones with clotted cream.

'It's so good of you to have us,' the older one said. 'I'm still puzzled as to how you found out about us.'

'Well, I know you've been through some painful times recently,' Miss Dodd said. 'But let me assure you, the cause of that pain, a certain Mark Joplin, is due for a very rude shock.'

And to the delight of Beth and Margot, she told the story of how she'd had Mark followed to the offices of a lawyer, how she surmised his purpose in going there, and how she'd given the same lawyer instructions to prepare a deed for the sale of Mark's house. A detective she'd hired had found that Mark lived very comfortably in an expensive home that he tried to keep a secret, built no doubt from the misery of others.

'In the end,' she told them, 'it was his bladder that led to his downfall. When he left the room leaving me to sign, I simply switched his set of deeds with the set I'd had prepared, and was signing mine when he hurried in to sign them and get away as quickly as he could. I was lucky that he thought it proper to sign in my presence, and hadn't signed the ones he gave me already. The letterhead was identical, so his suspicions weren't aroused. He didn't stop to examine the contents a second time.'

With that, she reached under a cushion of the three-seater lounge and pulled out the folder with Mark's deeds. The two women clapped and giggled.

'In a day or two, the truth will out,' she said, 'but it will be too late for Mark Joplin. Survival of the fittest. Part of my reason in inviting you here, ladies, is to let you know that I'll be using some of my ill-gotten gains to make sure you are paid in full, and a little more to make up for the hurt.'

The three women embraced each other, and as Beth and Margot crossed the road to their cars, Mark, this time with tortured emotion, was telling a concerned middle-aged woman a kilometre away about the costs of chemotherapy.

Roger

'We made the trip to Madang every fortnight in a small, single-engine Cessna.' Roger fixed me with a look I'd later learn was the intense one he adopted for the small repertoire of stories he never doubted people found captivating. 'You can get to the mainland from Karkar by boat, but it's much quicker by plane.'

'Roger!' Rosa interrupted with an authority that matched Roger's storytelling passion. 'This is our new neighbour's first visit, and I can't fathom why, after thirty-five years, everyone we meet has to hear of your plane crash. There's a time and a place, after all. Don't you agree, Ron?'

It wouldn't be the last time I'd be caught between the two of them in a tug-of-war. I looked from one to the other. 'Well, I hope you didn't sustain any serious injuries, Roger.' I steered a middle course that pleased him, mindful of Rosa moving slowly, hampered by her troublesome hip, towards the intricately carved occasional table next to the chair where I was sitting, with a small tray of olives, pâté, small square bites of toast, and sundried tomato.

'The three of us were over the Bismarck Sea, approaching the mainland. It was a fine day, we'd done all the required checks, and there was no turbulence,' Roger continued, 'when suddenly the engine…'

'Roger, our guest will think we're being very rude. Don't you think you should offer Ron a drink?' Rosa was determined that decorum be observed. 'And I'll have a champagne.'

'Champagne, Ron?' Roger was thrown off his stride, but determined to keep his composure.

I asked if they had ginger ale, and as Roger, briefly subdued, searched his bar fridge, and Rosa, the attentive hostess, nudged the tray of hors d'oeuvre closer, I was able to look around the apartment that was immediately above my own in the unit block.

Apart from the clutter, there were heavy, ornately carved wooden chests in the hallway, a number of neck-high carved statues in dark wood, one of a woman with tubular breasts that hung to her navel, and several amateurish paintings that looked like dusky Gauguins, all of unsmiling natives with large fleshy lips. They could have been painted with tinctured clay, and seemed out of place among the rest of the conventional furniture. I later wondered if they'd been painted and carved by the natives on the coffee plantation in Karkar that Roger managed with his brother.

'Please help yourself, Ron,' Rosa said solicitously, regaining her specially padded seat by the window. I would learn later that at eighty-two, she was three years older than Roger, yet her hair was still predominantly dark and her face relatively free of wrinkles. She looked eastern European, could have been Jewish, yet spoke cultivated English with a hint of affectation, yet without the suggestion of an accent. She was tiny, well rounded, and sitting in her window chair, her knees seemed to protrude from her midriff with no observable thigh.

'The engine stopped,' Roger continued, remembering where he'd left off, as he approached with my glass of ginger ale.

I already wondered if my failure to appreciate the expensive champagne had damaged my reputation as the neighbour to cultivate.

He wore shorts, and his legs were the size of tree trunks, albeit white, soft and hairless. His head hair was uniformly sparse, and as I would also later learn, his large pot belly and general mien of a life well-lived, even a decadent one, did not interfere with his assumed sex appeal for women of all ages.

'There was no explanation. They never found out why. Only conjecture,' he said, handing me my ginger ale, and peering at his hopefully captive audience of one through his bifocals, before he returned to his seat with a fistful of toast bites and sundried tomato.

'We hit the water with an almighty bang, and the plane straight away began to sink. I think I was unconscious for a few seconds.' This was apparently the part that Roger relished. The tempo of his voice increased. 'Pain, you've no idea. I knew I was badly hurt. I could barely move. Really thought it was the end.'

'Roger, whatever happened to the party pies? They were in the oven.'

'I ate them,' he said testily. 'Can I finish my story?'

'All of them? But there were twelve of them twenty minutes ago.'

'I managed to free myself from the cockpit. Struggled to stay afloat. To find something to grab hold of. A wing, a wheel. Anything. Eighty foot of water.'

'Some more pâté, Ron,' Rosa whispered.

I wondered if the whisper was an indication that even she was reluctant to stop Roger when he was at his impassioned height. But her interruption didn't go unnoticed by Roger.

'The result...' he resumed quietly. The desired climax had been so diminished, it was no longer a climax. The story was spoiled, but he had no option but to finish. 'Two broken legs, a fractured shoulder and a punctured lung. A steel plate here,' and he pulled up his shorts to reveal a faint scar in the fig softness of his thigh. 'Four months in hospital.' He quickly left the room, not looking at either Rosa or myself.

All was silence. The wooden statues and fleshy-lipped natives seemed to be staring at me with witchcraft-like intentions. For a moment, the room was eerie.

'He won't be back,' Rosa sighed. 'Welcome to the Middletons, Ron.'

And of the dozens of times I visited the Middletons over the next few years, often to enquire about Rosa's increasing discomfort with her hip, this would be a common scenario, even when I was invited by Roger, hoping that I could comfort Rosa. That, and Roger's shouting in arguments with Rosa that echoed around the entire unit block, followed by the slamming of doors.

I'd moved to my apartment six years ago and lived alone. While unit life had some restrictions, there was ample opportunity for anonymity. Tenants came and left, though a small group of elderly single women did patrol the grounds on most days, retailing gossip and on the look out for owner and tenant transgressions that threatened the sanctity of the property. Roger was always at odds with these women, all of them convinced of their weatherproof rightness.

In the years that I knew the Middletons, Roger bought two new cars, each with a price tag of over a quarter of a million, and a large yacht that he paid to have sailed from its moorings in Perth. All these purchases, and the newest in phone and computer technologies, were purchased without Rosa's knowledge, though Roger was quick to indicate that he had done it for her alone, a constantly argued reason that incensed her. He never used the boat, and it was sold at a considerable loss. The cars were eventually traded for something more basic.

My own relationship with Roger was one of forced tolerance. As chairperson of the unit strata, I would often be accosted as I returned home from work exhausted in the afternoons to be confronted before I opened my door with his demands that I call the strata manager about tenants not using the labelled rubbish bins, his proposal that the width of a path be widened to accommodate wheelchair access, and his plans for an inclinator for Rosa who was finding mobility an increasing problem. I could never understand why he wouldn't phone himself.

I was particularly concerned by the scurrilous emails he sent to my school email address about Muslims and gays. He believed both to be the scourge of the world. I told him on a number of occasions that I found these sentiments offensive, but it made no difference. And yet I still believe there was no malice in the man. He was simply unaware, unable to free himself from the tangled web of his extraordinary self-centredness.

In weekends, I'd often pass him at the nearby shops where he'd go for a secret breakfast or lunch before he returned home to the breakfast or lunch that Rosa had prepared for him. I'd sometimes pass coffee shops where he'd be sitting, often next to an unsuspecting woman, and I'd hear catches of phrases, 'nosedived', 'the Bismarck sea', 'two broken legs'.

On one occasion, when he didn't visit the shops for several weeks, I surmised, perhaps unfairly, that his public condemnation of Muslims and gays might have been greeted with hostility or threats. He certainly wasn't in tune with social mores. One of the neighbours reported that she heard him greeting a young woman he passed in the street, a complete stranger, telling her she had 'great boobies'.

*

He knocked on my door at ten-thirty one night. The conventional times that govern most of our lives meant little to him, and I had to scramble to dress.

'Rosa's in so much pain,' he said, looking forlorn. 'You could cheer her up,' and he began to cry. 'She's had such a hard life. Lost both her parents in the bombing of Germany during the war,' and he related her emigration to Australia as a young girl. 'She's probably never told you,' he said, 'but as a little girl she was chosen to present Hitler with a bouquet of flowers.' Rosa later confirmed the truth of this remark.

We're often surprised by new realities. Some of us must be very incomplete jigsaws, at least for others, with so many missing pieces. I thought of Rosa, tiny and balled uncomfortably in her window chair, and the smooth, pale-skinned little girl, perhaps with her hair in pigtails, tentatively offering the flowers to the Führer. I also saw the ravings of a lunatic to an adoring crowd, and thousands of regimented soldiers goose-stepping.

And I saw Roger, in tears as he recounted her history. We all thought their relationship internecine, yet something maintained them in their constant state of war. The origin of our needs is so often a mystery. Perhaps a life together, however hostile, is better than being alone.

There was a long pause after he finished, and I felt the need to reassure, or at least to say something optimistic.

'Life can teach us so much,' I said, and instantly felt like a pedant. 'Strength often springs from tragedy. Rosa must have spent a lot of time thinking about what happened to her, and arriving at insights because of it. I'll bet she's a very wise woman.'

Roger remained silent, but seemed pleased by my mention of Rosa's wisdom.

'The Greeks were very critical of the unexamined life,' I continued, thinking it a suitable time to talk about the importance of being aware of other people's needs, at the same time wondering if he'd understand the classical references to an ancient culture.

'Well, it's all Greek to me,' he retorted, pleased with himself. 'What is there to examine? Live and let live.'

I rang Rosa while he sat quietly, and asked if she would like to see me. She didn't know where Roger was, queried my choice of time with some irritation, and said she was too tired for company. It was another all-too-familiar scenario.

*

I remember the date. The seventh of April in the ninth year of my being in the apartment, and the day my uncle Wally died. He was a loud and extroverted man, and the life of the party as long as he was able to keep the 'life' within acceptable limits. He was likeable, red-faced and rugose, his bonhomie sustained by drink. Yet behind the masquerade were hints of family bitterness that mocked his public cheer and made victims in his sacred home, no doubt the day-long aftermath of excessive drinking.

He went upstairs to sleep one summer's afternoon, and never did wake up. There'd been no warning.

I didn't see much of Wally, so it was challenging more than distressing for me, the all-too-frequent reminder of our fragility, another step along mortality's linear pathway to death, and because we are diminished a little with every death.

When I was invited to visit Roger and Rosa the night of the funeral, it didn't escape Rosa's attention that I was more subdued than normal.

'Are you a little down in the dumps?' she asked without apparent empathy.

'A little flat,' I answered. 'A painful experience today.' I was of course referring to the show of grief at the funeral, and didn't mean to be dramatic in my choice of words.

'Pain! I'll tell you what pain is,' Roger called from across the room. 'Pain is trying to force a cockpit door open against tons of rushing water with two legs that don't work, and agony in a busted chest. Pain is having your life flash before your eyes, and trying to tread water when your body's broken. That's what pain is.'

'Shut up, Roger,' Rosa threatened, but she didn't enquire further, and we sat through a rare half-minute of silence before I made excuses and left.

I could hear them shouting as I made my way down the stairs. A few moments later, a door slammed.

Once inside, I used the internet to research Changi and Sandarkan, grim horrors with many hidden scars that might have launched Wally's flight from privation and cruelty to a drunken thirst that never could be quenched, a voluntary insanity. I wondered if Wally felt he had to live his own domesticated Changi, his mere survival forfeiting the right to lasting peace.

So where is the fabled line in the sand that marks 'enough', the line defining the limits of hurt people can inflict on each other and still be excused? Is there a private history that mitigates a crime or any inflicted pain for that matter, or a perpetrator's state of mind that excuses the harm they cause?

If there is such a line, such a history, is Roger any different? Of course he hasn't suffered at all. Certainly not in the way Wally had. He was born with a silver spoon in his mouth, and yet he irritates us all. What causes him to be the bête noire of virtually everyone he meets? Is his behaviour less defensible than Wally's because he has never really suffered? If only we could read the secret history of those who abuse us. Of course there are some who rise from the ashes like the phoenix, and others who sink into them.

*

Once we were over the shock of Roger's new accident, and had received news that he would survive, though probably be in hospital for a couple of months, there was some light-heartedness, probably a nervous reaction to near tragedy.

'It'll be stories of the four-wheel drive that hit him now, and not that bloody plane,' a neighbour commented with a titter of approval from others.

I had to smile myself, imagining Roger holding up his hand to halt the car speeding towards him, like Canute ordering the waves to recede.

I visited him with Rosa the day after his first operation. She was by this time barely mobile; she had never learned to drive. And of course they had few friends. Their only son was still in Papua New Guinea and, despite much toing and froing on the phone, he hadn't come home to support his mother.

'It's Mr Middleton's wife,' a nurse said to the sister in charge, and I couldn't help but notice the warning look. 'Watch out,' it seemed to say.

Seeking the sister's confidence while Roger complained to Rosa, I learned that he was an impossible patient. He had already accused his surgeon of incompetence, and demanded 'the best man in the field'. He made constant and unrealistic demands of the nurses, and some inappropriate comments. The look she gave me left little doubt as to the nature of the comments.

After he had given Rosa an exhaustive list of 'dos', including the

137

search for doctors and lawyers whose credentials could be investigated, we said our goodbyes.

'Bring her back tomorrow morning,' he said to me, though not unpleasantly.

'But Roger,' I replied, 'I have school. I have to work. I can't come every day. I'll bring Rosa on Thursday after school.'

He turned away as if insulted.

'Perhaps a taxi,' I ventured. 'Or there must be others who…' and I saw Rosa shake her head.

After six weeks of great endurance for Rosa and myself, not to mention the harassed doctors and nurses, Roger was given the first indication of imminent release.

'You have to be delighted,' I said, sitting on the end of his bed. 'Do you think it's changed you?' I asked, feeling he might want to share any insights that flowed from his pain. Dramatic or even just new experiences are often the source of growing, and often of resolution, if we allow them to be.

'What is there to learn?' he answered mockingly, affecting incredulity. ' I had an accident. I survived. Nothing's changed. I'm going home.'

I chastised myself for asking. I should have known better. There'd been no traction for his primitive philosophy.

*

He'd only been home for three months, making our lives impossible, when he died. His death was sudden. Like Wally, he simply didn't wake up one morning, and the doctors assured us his demise wasn't related to the injuries caused by the accident.

Rosa was philosophical, if an unquestioning acceptance merits the status of a philosophy. She must have known it meant that she would either be placed in a nursing home, or live with the family of the adopted son, who arrived to make final arrangements. I never found out what happened to her.

The funeral was at St Augustine's, the local Anglican church, though neither Roger nor Rosa had ever been worshippers. Pristine and Omo-white White Ladies, tasteful with maroon relief, arranged the service for a meagre number who arrived in snivelling rain. The service was short and impersonal. Only the minister spoke. And as the rain beat against the dour stained glass where Mary, fractured between a network of lead, gave succour to the baby Jesus, the few fraying knots of mourners thought of washing getting wet on the line, the roast in the oven, or the need to collect children from school.

I shook hands with the son, thanked the minister, whose words were obviously used generally to apply to those departed who had no one to extol their merits (I thought I might have been asked), and kissed Rosa whose only concern now was her son.

We left the church slowly, hampered by Rosa's slow pace. There were no tears. No wake.

The thought of what came next had neither daunted nor intrigued Roger. I'd never heard him express a purpose for his years, or wonder about the meaning of the universe. Apart from the physical limits of his world and the three-bedroom apartment he shared with Rosa in a perpetual state of conflict, he had never sussed out a less temporal place to call his own. It may have been just as well I wasn't asked to speak. What could I have said?

Outside, it was still raining, and though we were not on any flight path, the sound of an engine from a light plane, invisible beyond the dark cloud and rain, was unmistakeable. Rosa looked up to the heavens and rolled her eyes.

Green-eyed Monster

'Two Pats. That'll be a bit different on the wedding invitations,' Mr Mannering said, helping himself to another roast potato under the watchful eyes of his wife.

'I stopped being Pat when I was eight, Dad. Ever since then, it's been Trish. Trish Mannering,' his daughter replied.

'You were christened Patricia,' Mrs Mannering said peremptorily, 'and that's what it will say on the wedding invites! The marriage of Patricia Catherine Mannering and Patrick Ian Styles.'

Patrick, sensing tension between mother and daughter, was quick to defuse possible conflict. 'She's Trish to everyone now, but I'm sure there's no problem with Patricia on the wedding invitations.'

'More wine, Trevor,' Ruth Mannering ordered her husband. 'Patrick's glass has been empty for ten minutes.'

'I've done very well, Mrs Mannering.' Patrick attempted a lame defence of his future father-in-law. 'Water's all I need now. Don't want to disgrace myself in front of my future in-laws,' he added to lighten the mood.

'It might be easier if you call me Trevor from now on,' Mr Mannering said. 'What do you think, Ruth?' He looked at his wife appealingly. 'Christian names for both of us?'

'I'll need to think about it,' Ruth Mannering answered stonily.

'Mum!' Trish reacted with a hint of hostility. 'What's to think about?'

'Clear away the dishes, Trevor, and I'll get the dessert.' Ruth Mannering decided to ignore her daughter's protest. She was an impressive looking middle-aged woman with dark brown, cropped hair, immaculately groomed and made-up, and a no nonsense bearing that seemed to belie an impassive beauty.

'Yes, dear,' Trevor Mannering answered obligingly, and scraped the plates to collect while Ruth Mannering signalled to Patrick to sit down when he'd stood up to help.

His father-in-law to-be seemed older than his wife, but that was probably because of his premature greying and balding. He had a kind face and eyes that always expressed the emotion he felt all too readily.

With dessert came a discussion of wedding plans, with the family matriarch asking her daughter questions and asserting her own definite opinions. Talk of the wedding dress, flowers for the church, the cake, and what the bridesmaids would wear, was considered by the men to be women's business.

'I do hope you'll wear your hair up,' Ruth Mannering urged. 'It's so unruly when you have it down. I'll get Mrs Glassop to do it for you. And you can tell Yvette, I assume she's the bridesmaid, that Mrs Glassop can do hers to match. You've no idea, Patrick, how hard it is for me to get her to spend time on how she looks.'

'I'm sure she'll look beautiful, Mrs Mannering,' Patrick answered. 'Even more beautiful than she is tonight,' he felt the need to add to redress the criticism.

'I'm sure you're right, Patrick. I hope we'll all be proud of her. Ever since she was a little girl she wasn't interested in the things other girls were interested in. Looking pretty wasn't at the top of the list, was it, darling?' She looked at her daughter with obvious affection. 'I'll never forget how you'd play in the mud when you were a little one. Trevor, I hope you turned the percolator on.'

'All under control, dear,' Trevor answered benignly, bringing the coffee cups to the table.

'She's just overanxious,' Trish said to Patrick when they were alone after the meal. 'It's really important to her, how everyone looks and behaves. And particularly how she looks. She'll be shattered if it doesn't go off without a hitch.'

Patrick nodded but didn't speak, thinking of the dinner-time conversation.

'Not having second thoughts, are you?' Trish teased, putting her arm around his shoulders.

'For better or worse, my love,' Patrick grinned. 'I'm not letting you get away.'

*

Friendship sometimes emerges from a kind act by a near stranger. Of course, the act might come from covert admiration or attraction. This was how it was for Patrick and Trish.

Patrick had been teaching year six at a large primary school for two years when Trish was appointed to the school to teach year three. At a staff meeting towards the end of the first week, an older woman teaching the same stage as Trish, whose twenty years of teaching experience was really one year repeated twenty times, criticised the inadequate programs of the younger teachers. Everyone noticed her looking at Trish.

After a few seconds of embarrassed silence, Trish, feeling mortified, observed a young man of average height with pale blue eyes and a slightly receding hairline, stand to speak.

'I don't know about the other teachers, but I've seen Trish Mannering's programs,' he said, 'and they are outstanding. I certainly couldn't do better, and by the way,' he continued, 'I don't think this is the forum for being publicly critical of other teachers.'

His remarks were greeted by a chorus of 'hear hears' and 'bravo.'

Trish thanked him afterwards. They'd never spoken before, though she knew him by reputation. His affability made him well liked by the students and other teachers.

'But you've never seen my programs,' she said.

'Haven't I?' he replied with exaggerated surprise, and grinned.

That was the beginning.

Trish was unmistakeably her mother's daughter but, while attractive, she didn't have her mother's conventional beauty. It was a battle to keep the curls in her sandy hair neat, but the adolescent freckles that had once so irked her mother had disappeared, blended with her pale honey complexion. And her mother had helped her lose the teenage puppy fat that had lingered into her maturer years.

It was a whirlwind romance. Convention usually decrees a lengthy 'getting to know you' period, to guard against hasty marriages that will end in regret. These interludes are more typically 'getting to know yourself' times, personal development, and opportunities to come to grips with the prospect or reality of mutual living. But Trish and Patrick had no doubt about being ready.

From the time of their first meeting, there were still summer and early autumn months of warm weather, and they were both beach lovers. It wasn't far for them to travel, so most weekends were spent at one of the local beaches, liberated from the constraints of teaching. They swam, splashed each other with the ocean water like children, buried each other in the sand, and sunbaked, fondling and stealing kisses.

'Patrick,' she said warningly once. 'You're ogling that girl.'

'Ogling,' he queried. 'I looked at her. You have to admit,' he continued without embarrassment, 'she looks great in that bikini. She must go to the gym.'

'And what about this little lady here in her black bikini,' Trish answered teasingly, playing the seductress and kissing him, before rolling over silently on her back.

It seemed appropriate that Patrick's proposal came as they walked the length of the beach in burning sun, waist-deep in still water at Church Point. They were more in awe than exhilarated. They knew it was the natural conclusion, but it was still momentous for both of them.

The wedding was everything Mrs Mannering wanted, and she remained Mrs Mannering for Patrick rather than 'Ruth' or 'Mum'.

Trish allowed Mrs Glassop to do her hair in the style her mother requested, and met with her mother's critical approval.

'You look a picture for once,' she said. 'I'm so glad you allowed me some say in the dresses for you and Yvette.'

The married couple had a brief honeymoon in Fiji before returning to school.

*

'Two tickets to the opera, *Aida*,' Trish gloomily told Yvette. 'I found them in the pocket of his jacket. You know how expensive they are?'

They were sitting in a café where they met every fortnight for coffee and catch-up.

Yvette, tall, hazel-eyed, and erring on the side of thin, did not share her friend's pessimism. 'But Trish,' she said dismissively, 'why do you think they're for someone else? He might be wanting to keep it a secret and give you a surprise.'

'He's not one for surprises.' Trish remained sullen. 'He'd have told me by now. Since I found them, I've asked a couple of times if we might go to a play or a show, and he acted dumb. No. Yvette, he's taking another woman. Three months, three months married. Didn't take long, did it?'

'I think you're being premature Trish,' Yvette countered. 'There could be any number of explanations.'

'I think he's interested in other women,' Trish said after a brief pause. 'You should see how he carries on with the school secretary. He calls her gorgeous, and they flirt outrageously. I know, I just know they like each other. And he's always sizing up other women, especially on the beach. It makes me feel as if I'm not good enough.'

Believing Trish was being unreasonable, Yvette sprang to Patrick's defence, admitted that a little jealousy was not a bad thing as long as it was kept within reasonable limits, and assured her that Patrick only had eyes for her.

'Am I attractive, Yvette?' Trish asked, and quickly changed the question. 'I mean, do you really think he loves me?'

Yvette was taken by surprise. 'Of course he loves you, and yes, you are a very attractive woman.'

Patrick was home when she returned from the café, and taking him firmly by the hand, a woman with a mission rather than with tenderness, she led him to the family room and ordered him to sit down. 'All right,' she began aggressively, 'who are you taking to the opera?'

'I beg your pardon?' Patrick looked surprised.

'Don't play the innocent with me, Patrick,' she continued, 'I've seen the tickets. Who is she? I hope it's not Clara from school. That really would be embarrassing.'

The light suddenly dawned for Patrick. 'Trish,' he said, 'Rod and Belinda Briggs ordered the tickets online, and they had to be picked up in person at the Opera House. I had to be at Circular Quay for the leaders' conference and offered to collect the tickets for them. They gave me the identification I needed to do so.'

Trish seemed deflated but still unconvinced. 'You're telling me they're not your tickets.'

Patrick was finding it difficult to conceal his anger. 'Did you look at the dates, because if you did, you would have realised that it's the weekend we're away visiting your parents!'

'Well, you can't blame me.' Trish was embarrassed but not yet fully contrite. 'You have an interest in other women that's…that's unhealthy. Sometimes I think you don't love me any more. I love you, Patrick,' she said with childlike candour, and in lieu of apology.

Patrick retreated before Trish began to cry, and went for a run, nursing his hurt. She'd made comments about him looking at other women on the beach, but he assumed they were light-hearted, or an innocent way of fishing for compliments. He thought she shared in his comical flirtation with Clara at school.

'I love you, Patrick,' she'd said with big eyes beginning to fill with water. I suppose that's true, he thought, and felt a fleeting comfort. But he knew that jealousy isn't about too much love. It's more about insecurity. I'll do all I can to make her feel important, he decided.

It had been their first real disagreement, and as he returned breathing heavily from his run, he resolved that this lover's quarrel would not be damaging. It would be a renewal of their love.

*

'I felt really bad after that business with the tickets,' Trish confided in Yvette at their café rendezvous. 'It's a terrible feeling while it lasts, and afterwards you have to deal with the shame and self-hate. Anyway, I hope I've learned a lesson.'

'I read somewhere that jealousy is about compare and despair,' Yvette replied, 'that a jealous woman thinks someone else is better than she is. Trish, Trish,' and she reached out and took her friend's hand, 'you are a very attractive woman. It's the others who don't compare. Believe me, you have nothing to worry about.'

'You're a real friend, Yvette,' Trish answered. 'I think I believe that. I do believe that!'

'That's the girl! You have to believe it, Trish. Patrick's a good man, and you don't want to risk losing him.'

'I can tell you one good thing about it,' Trish said cheekily as they paid to leave, 'it was great fun making up.'

At the end of the third school term, teachers were asked to remain after school to farewell a teacher who was retiring after seventeen years at the same school. The support staff had organised a lavish afternoon tea, and sixty teachers gathered around the tables with sugar stickying the creases from overstuffed mouths.

A rattle of spoon on glass school-belled formality and the principal began.

'It's forty years since Bob began,' the recipe as old as that for scones: the shallow history, the would-be funny retirement quotes, 'but seriously, though,' and thoughts commuted in time as teachers wondered what words could capture their life, what parting insight might squeeze a tear.

The conventional gift unnerved and the expected jesting as Bob replied, dulled to catalogue of thanks. The women fairy-clapped, juggling cups of tea.

An exuberant Clara, made merrier by the permitted alcohol, was flirting innocently with some of the male teachers, but when she approached Patrick, was pushed away by Trish. She stumbled but quickly regained her balance.

'Keep your hands off my husband,' Trish warned with pursed lips.

The room was suddenly silent. Everyone turned to observe.

'No problem,' Clara said, feigning gaiety, but escaping hurriedly and red-faced through the throng of colleagues.

Patrick also tried to make light of the situation. Better that than make an issue of it. But he couldn't wait till they could take their leave with a shred of dignity. He wrestled to contain his fury till they got home.

'Well, what was that all about?' he asked, trying to conceal his anger.

'She's a flirt. Surely you can see that,' Trish attacked. 'Let her flirt with other men, but not my husband.'

'Trish,' Patrick tried to mollify, 'she means no harm. It's all innocent fun. It's not as if she's trying to get her claws into me, or any of the others.'

But Trish wouldn't be appeased. 'Perhaps she wouldn't be like that if you men stopped encouraging her. It's obvious you really like her, and she really likes you. Why don't you get together?'

Patrick's run, a therapy of sorts, did nothing to quell his anger. Fear of rejection was one thing. Public humiliation was another. He would have to return to the school next term, and he knew that tongues would have been wagging furiously. When he returned from his run, Trish was subdued and apologetic, but passionate renewal was the furthest thing from his mind.

Everything was calm, even loving for a few weeks, until the Briggses came to dinner.

'How was *Aida*?' Patrick asked as they entered, accepting the bottle of wine that Rod proffered.

'Wonderful,' Belinda answered. 'Thank you so much for getting the tickets. You're a darling. It saved me a trip to the city.' And before sitting down, she hugged him for a second, kissing him on the cheek.

Trish said nothing. But she didn't have to. She was surly for the rest of the evening, avoiding conversation with ill grace, answering questions brusquely when asked, and even banging the dishes in the kitchen.

'Another of your admirers,' she said sarcastically when the Briggses had left.

*

Patrick received a few odd looks when he returned to school for the fourth term, but nothing was said. Things had mercifully moved on, though Clara was very circumspect and he missed her good cheer that had always brightened his days. He found himself becoming resentful that Trish had created this unsmiling formality.

His relationship with Trish had suffered, though he held onto hope that time would be the great healer. He began to distrust his natural affable self, believing Trish might find fault. Colleagues noted the subtle difference in his withdrawal.

Trish was aware of what she had done, and even initiated talks with him, intent to explain how the feeling consumed her, and how she found it difficult to deal with the residual shame. The talks always ended in tears and brought them closer, sometimes ending in intimacy. But Patrick remained on tenterhooks.

The leadership conferences included those school personnel who currently occupied leadership roles, and focused on the development of skills. Patrick had been to the first, but two others were to follow, with sufficient time between them to enable participants to practise what they'd learned.

The usual format involved a principal or academic from a university giving input on an aspect of leadership, and then the participants forming groups to discuss set questions and report back. Group membership was organised so that the groups were different for each of the three meetings, enabling teachers and administrators from numerous schools to network.

Attending the second conference, Patrick found the lecture input particularly boring, and the general reaction to such a colourless presentation was a light-heartedness in his newly formed group. They laughed a lot, and he formed a real connection with Bianca, a deputy principal from a nearby school, a woman with pillar-box-red lips and nails, and a permanently mischievous look. They infected the other group members with their satire, and the peels of laughter provoked the concern of the department's course organisers. Patrick was reminded of the fun he'd had with Clara, and began to feel alive again.

When the afternoon tea break was over, and before the course wash-up began, Bianca took his arm. 'Let's get out of here, Patrick,' she said.

Patrick didn't hesitate, even though he wasn't sure what Bianca had in mind. Was 'getting out of here' code for 'let's go somewhere we can be alone'? Was it a proposition? No, surely not. It didn't matter anyway. Trish had made up her mind he was sleeping with other women. And he felt attracted to Bianca. She was a free spirit.

*

Three other staff members at the school had attended the conference, so Patrick's escape with an animated companion soon became known. Trish avoided him at school after she heard the news, but exploded when they arrived home.

'I've been right all along,' she shouted. 'Who else have you been sleeping with?'

'Trish, I didn't…'

'Don't you dare Trish me, you, you…monster. And you talk of public humiliation. How am I going to face them at school? Won't they have a lovely time with their gossip. What a hypocrite.'

'Are you going to let me explain?' Patrick tried to reason.

'No, I'm not. There's nothing you can say. Nothing!' Trish was adamant. 'This marriage is over.'

Yvette tried to soothe Trish when she arrived at her flat that evening with an overnight bag, sobbing. 'But what did the teachers say?' Yvette urged. 'They left together but that's all they know, and it's all you know. Why think the worst?'

'She was beautiful, they all said. Full of fun.'

'Trish, I don't believe for a moment that Patrick cheated. He's always been loyal. You haven't given him a chance to tell his side of the story.'

'You've heard what they said,' Trish was dismissive. 'She was better-looking than me. Well, he can have this Bianca woman for all I care.'

'Bianca? Bianca Stone?' Yvette was suddenly inquisitive. 'Deputy principal at Erina West?'

'That's her. Why? You know her?' Trish was accusing.

'Trish,' Yvette began quietly, 'I've known Bianca for years, and I can assure you beyond a shadow of a doubt that Patrick did not cheat on you. Bianca has altogether different sexual preferences, if you know what I mean. The worst thing Patrick has done is to have a drink with her.'

Trish was suddenly quiet, leant forward and buried her head in her hands. 'What have I done?' she wailed. 'I can't face him tonight. I'll go home in the morning.'

When morning came, Trish asked if she could stay with Yvette for another day. It was Saturday and she was feeling too fragile to face Patrick so soon after her cruel outburst of the afternoon before. Emotionally exhausted, she asked if she could return to her bed for the morning.

Yvette, after mulling over the idea of visiting Patrick to prepare the way for Trish's return by trying to defend her reaction, decided she would go. It could do no further harm.

But when Patrick opened the door, all she could manage was an emotionally charged 'I'm so sorry, Patrick.'

Standing in the doorway, they held each other gently like fine china for a few seconds, and Yvette kissed him, a mere brush of moist lips on his cheek. As they let go, they looked at each other curiously at arm's length as if seeing the other for the first time. Yvette's lips were trembling.

A Matter of Blame

It was sudden, but not sought. At least not at first, and not consciously. Their compulsive need for each other wasn't just the frolic of hormones, though that did take over when opportunity smiled through the urgent signals from their eyes and words. Such need usually begins with our personal histories as we sift through the encounters and possibilities that life throws up, and that prepare us or propel us towards action.

That was what they thought in different ways as they lay naked together, stilled on her marital bed, she flushed with the rosy warmth that comes after exertion, and he with a satisfied look and a light sheen of perspiration.

'Wow' from him, and her near-bemused laugh spoke for the awesomeness of what had just occurred. 'Did what I think just happen?' he asked.

She nodded with a conspiratorial wink, and they both smiled gleefully like children who had escaped from stealing fruit from a neighbour's orchard.

Such a landmark event gathers its own mythology. In the months that followed, as they grew to know each other better, they tried to explain it by history. His attempt was more a dissection, an exacting and sometimes trenchant examination of his recent years. Hers was a less exacting and more emotional criticism of the limitations of her marriage.

In light-hearted moments, they'd cast mock blame, accusing the other of deliberate seduction.

'It was all your doing,' she'd say.

'I didn't have a chance. I was attacked,' he'd retaliate.

'From what I remember, you didn't put up much of a fight.'

And this repartee continued throughout the relationship.

They settled for an impartial reality. He wasn't the prevalent male, and she wasn't the scarlet woman. Their need was mutual, fuelled by alcohol, phoney party talk, the games people play, and couples pressed together in erotic clinches. A vision of emptiness that needed an antidote.

He fetched her a drink. They sat together. He wasn't smitten. Neither was she. The talk began with a shared commentary on some of the partygoers. She was critical of the superficiality and conceit of the women in particular. He condemned the games being played between the sexes as one person tried to impress another. Empathy grew with the aphrodisiac of talk, and as chemistry worked its magic.

The decision to leave was later imputed to the other.

'I'm sure it was you who said let's get out of here,' she quipped. 'I think you had designs on me even then.'

'But we ended up at your house,' he'd counter. 'Your house,' he repeated with emphasis, as if that was certain proof. 'How do you explain that?'

Her husband was interstate at a business conference, the reason for her not having a companion at the party. What followed later was a scenario enacted in that same bedroom many times to come.

But there was no instant grappling. Neither expected it yet, and propriety demanded a preamble. Defences were weak but a certain dignity had to be preserved. Polite formality over coffee and toast, and a brief recounting of each other's background relaxed further to a hug in the kitchen as he cleared the cups and plates.

Most approaching actions are reversible, yet they both later agreed that the line had been crossed. Yet again they blithely accused the other.

'You started it all. You kissed me first.'

'OK then, but even if that's true, who took my hand and led me upstairs?'

She had never been unfaithful before. He had never slept with a married woman.

'It was somehow bigger than both of us,' she'd say later that night as an excuse, and later still to sanction the meetings that followed, as they swapped the clichés of how it was better than anything they'd ever known.

He didn't stay the night, even though it was safe to do so. He felt strangely naked for the first time as he dressed in the dark, trembling a little, though it wasn't cold. He may have been surprised by the suddenness of it all. Perhaps decency had been sufficiently flouted, or time was needed to take stock. As she lay on her side, a wash of moonlight from a gap in the curtains gambolled about her buttocks and thighs, making them gleam like satin.

She reached out to him with both arms as he finished dressing, wanting him to stay, but accepting the decision. He leant over and kissed her while she tousled his hair.

Sudden. Dramatic. Impetuous. Unwise. They agreed. They also knew, without any discussion, that it would happen again. And again.

*

In drawing upon history as a reason, twenty-four-year-old bachelor Andrew Walker didn't give much credence to his childhood years. They were happy enough. No oedipal leanings, no unresolved crises that he was aware of.

He did lend some weight though to the impact of the church-based youth group that dominated his teenage years. It imposed a didactic morality, but one that was too uncertain of itself to be sanctimonious. He believed that history had been unkind. His adolescent years were a world of more stylised conventions. Emotion and desire were hemmed by inhibition. Egos were probably more fragile.

Sex, beyond the sanctioned limits, was frowned upon. In retrospect, he regretted not having been able to break free from these pious restraints. He'd recall several advances by girls that he realised now were full of sexual promise, but he was too naïve at the time to understand. Yet while he may have regretted being denied a more natural and fuller expression of feeling, he understood that he was as much a victim of his distinctive youth culture as of history. The moral convictions of that limited world, could be an enemy of the freedom he wanted.

In their heart-to-hearts, Andrew told Cindy that he was explaining his part in the relationship but not necessarily approving it. He felt the affair might be ill-advised but certainly not reprehensible. His considerations were more practical than moral, the danger of falling in love, and the hurt for all concerned if discovered.

For a couple of years before he met her at the party, he'd had a relationship of sorts with Gayle. It began with a telltale look across a room at a conference, followed by emotion's charge, but living in different states proved a challenge. Their love, if it could be called that, was kept alive by fantasies, and the promises he craved were slow to arrive. But self-denial was not strange for him.

'It's greater than the world,' she wrote, and in a rare moment of poetic dash, 'more than the earth, the skies and oceans.'

He returned her sentiments, claiming that he needed to touch and hold her, to know her as a man can truly know a woman. Of course he meant intimately.

As the days leaked into weeks, desire grew with despondency, and he resolved to go to her.

While her initial reasons to delay seemed plausible enough, compensated by the promised gifts of love, the excuses soon became weightless, floating in the wind like friable leaves.

Telling her that their love felt like an illusion, and that he needed to feel her body close to his own, her final answer was benign.

'Let's indulge the wonderful feelings we have for each other, and take pleasure in the rarity of our love,' she said. 'The earthy love you talk about is something we should rise above.'

He thought this weird, and the relationship, if it ever was one, ended abruptly.

It wasn't surprising that when Andrew met Cindy at that party, and he saw the artificial gesturing of the women, dangling their empty wine glasses like unchaste flowers, and the bravado of the men, lacking subtlety in their thirst for admiration, he longed for something real, not the false party world, not something ethereal, an unearthly love, and not something so inhibited it emasculated honest feeling. And honest desire.

He wasn't instantly attracted, but there was no pretension, and she spoke her own mind. She had an honesty, worldliness and forthrightness about her, and she seemed to understand his unusual history from the little he'd told her, though it was very different from her own.

He was hesitant when they'd returned to her house, felt a little like the bumbling adolescent, but she set him at ease, and when they'd crossed the line they often referred to, and she took his hand to lead him upstairs, a gesture so simple yet so charged with tender meaning, he had no doubts.

*

Cindy Furlong married at the age of twenty-one. She was six days younger than Andrew. The wedding was hurried, not the occasion she'd hoped for, because of her unwanted pregnancy. It would remain a source of resentment and, in her less rational moments, Malcolm would wear the blame. Ironically, she miscarried three weeks later.

She'd often wonder if things had been different, whether she would have married Malcolm at all. Choice of lifetime partner seemed so fickle.

She'd had two boyfriends before Malcolm, and both had excited her more, but that, she told herself, was a young girl's first taste of love, the requited die-for feeling that never goes away with time, but is embraced more reasonably, or soberly, and with greater understanding.

Edward was a ginger, bearded philosopher, studying at university, and living an alternative lifestyle. She liked his challenging of sacred cows, and they'd spend hours together talking of Rousseau and Thoreau, and creating their ideal world. He moved interstate and there was no further contact. Peter was a childhood sweetheart, and possessed the wholesomeness and image of 'the boy next door', even though he lived a few kilometres distant. Not all relationships end with drama. Theirs was a quiet fading away.

'I loved them both,' she'd later tell Andrew as sufficient reason for her intimacy with them, mindful of the contrast between her early adult life, and the prohibitions, often self-imposed, that dogged Andrew's.

She met Malcolm at the supermarket, and told her girlfriends to peals of laughter how their first, and she playfully called it 'romantic', exchange was over a packet of dog food. She thought little of the meeting, but she had given him sufficient information to be located, and he contacted her.

It was a quiet time in her life, having recently separated from Edward, and she was grateful for the attention. She found his unqualified love for her seductive, and he was attentive to her needs, sometimes so much that it was irritating. She felt that each little kindness was an implicit claim.

Giving herself after several months was not difficult. Doing so didn't have the mystique it did for Andrew. It was a natural part of growing intimacy whether or not the magic was there to welcome it.

She remembered the very day she must have conceived. She really couldn't blame him. It was as much her fault as his, but he was usually so responsible, and it irked her that this once he hadn't been.

Her miscarriage brought on a period of despondency, even though she hadn't really wanted the child. Not then anyway. Her thoughts turned inwards. She began to examine her life, questioning its meaning. And she shut Malcolm out.

She didn't deny him the sexual intimacy he craved, but she was unresponsive, and when he'd finished and rolled away, concerned that something was wrong, yet not daring to ask, she'd turn towards the window to the night sky pierced by stars, watch the fretting gum leaves cast reflections on the ceiling in the light cast by a meddling moon, and feel the loneliness of the room.

'You can talk to me, Cindy,' he told her reassuringly more than once.

But how could she tell him that he wouldn't understand, when she couldn't herself.

This was the time in her life she met Andrew. Malcolm was away at one of his many conferences, and while she didn't want to go to the party, she believed her girlfriend's advice that getting out would be good for her. She might not have been her usual animated self, but the quieter and more reflective Cindy found an ally in Andrew.

In their tender moments, Andrew would recall his abiding image of her taking his hand to lead him upstairs to something hopefully transcendent. She'd often thought about it too, without his prompting, weighing its layers of meaning, facing the world together, leaving a painful past, the promise of new beginnings, ascension. Malcolm hadn't figured in the reckoning.

*

Malcolm Berry didn't think the age difference mattered. If there was a concern, it wasn't that he was nine years older, but that she was nine years younger. She was only twenty, not an age that normally stamps one with maturity. Yet it soon became apparent that she was no novice in coping with the challenges life throws up.

'You have a lucky dog.' She'd taken him by surprise at the supermarket as he carried a large packet of dog food to the checkout.

'I hope he thinks so,' he answered, warming to her interest. 'No, I'm sure he does.'

'It is Lucky Dog, ' she said, and when he looked puzzled, 'The dog food,' and she pointed to the packet, 'is called Lucky Dog.'

'Oh.'

That was the beginning, at least for him. He later admitted to being taken with her there and then. You can't reason love, he'd later tell her. One of his friends kept introducing him to single women, some of whom ticked all the boxes. But love wasn't decided by inventories.

One of these potential partners was Caroline, a newly appointed thirty-year-old work colleague, whose violet eyes twinkled with an irony that matched her melody of laugh. Her apparent modesty was alluring for Malcolm, and during the months he took to ask her out, he nursed fictions of them exchanging deep and knowing looks, and silences between them that meant more than words. Of course there were erotic images as well.

Their first and only date was at a restaurant with his friends and their partners where he watched her tapping her cigarette ash while talking pretentiously, sitting with her skirt revealing the full length of both legs, perhaps a little more, and taking unconcealed delight as several of his male friends competed to buy her drinks.

Malcolm's fantasies were stricken. He heard the lost music of her voice, and watched her face reassemble from the sweetness he thought he knew, to something fake.

Cindy was different. No novice perhaps, but there was still freshness and honesty, a little girl's candour in asking a man about his dog. Pluses had been ticked off before for Malcolm. Other women would have scored higher for compatibility. But in affairs of the heart, that had little meaning.

So there was no hesitation in Malcolm's advances. He took her out, bought her gifts, actually enjoyed meeting her parents, and tried to meet her every need. He didn't press his claims too insistently, but waited till he thought the time was right. When, in moments of exasperation, she told him he was doing too much, that she didn't want to be feted so insistently, and even thought the attention was not normal, he listened without complaint. He found nothing in her that irritated him, like he had with Caroline, and his feeling grew, rather than diminished.

Although he asked her to move in with him, she remained living at home, where she shared an apartment with a girlfriend, and where he was a frequent visitor.

He knew her pregnancy would either make or break the relationship, and it caused him great anxiety. They'd spoken of children, but she had made it clear that in the event of their ever marrying, a family was years away. He wondered if this would spell the end.

The pregnancy didn't break the relationship, but it caused it to falter. She accepted his proposal at a time of indecision, and even though things between them improved, she harboured a resentment that a cloud had hovered over the wedding.

The miscarriage both united and divided them. It brought them together in sharing sadness, but checked their intimacy.

Malcolm held on tenaciously to the belief that her disappointment would eventually mellow into something even richer than they had before.

*

They were right in predicting that it would happen again. They'd usually meet at Andrew's, and sometimes at Cindy's when Malcolm was at one of his conferences and Cindy decided to cook. And it was always immediately after Malcolm had phoned from his conference hotel. It was a rare occasion that they went out together, usually to the theatre. It wasn't wise to be seen publicly.

Seldom was their lovemaking gentle. On these occasions, they might even profess their love, leaving them feeling a deep contentment. But there was never any discussion of a more meaningful future for them.

More often, the sex was a fury pounded frenziedly with little tenderness, perhaps a need to discover what they were searching for, or an analgesic deadening the sense of unsatisfied hope.

She'd usually stay the night if they were at his place and Malcolm was away. Andrew lived alone so it was safe to do so. If they were at her place, where there was always a little anxiety, however irrational, about being discovered, he'd often leave soon after, feeling that he was creeping away emptily from something momentous, yet, for the time being, spent. On these occasions, she'd feel a vague unease as if the means to fulfilment were only half realised. And if there was a moon, she'd watch the flickering on the ceiling till she fell asleep.

'What do you think he'd do if he found out?' Andrew asked, when they were speaking of Malcolm.

They were lying naked and damp on his bed, he on his side, and she supine, her hair a wild bush of auburn against the pillow, separate now that their lovemaking was complete.

'He'd kill me,' Cindy answered.

'But you keep saying he'd do anything for you,' Andrew persisted. 'So why wouldn't he forgive you?'

'Would you?'

They both knew it was a throwaway line, a senseless answer. They weren't husband and wife, and they both knew Malcolm's commitment to Cindy was greater than Andrew's.

Yet despite their refusal to commit to any future, they were jealous of each other having any other sexual partner. Cindy was concerned that Andrew, as a single man, was free to do what he liked.

'Is there something especially wicked in having the old married woman?' she'd ask teasingly, yet half seriously.

And Andrew needed constant reassurance that Malcolm's bedtime demands were infrequent and unsatisfying.

*

The night was clear and a full moon hung low in the sky. They lay together in her marital bed after her cooked meal of delicately spiced tagine lamb. Their lovemaking was tender. All was quiet except for the spawning frogs making clicking noises in the pond beneath the window. He'd later recall these inconsequential details, a way of checking the play of events he was sometimes tempted to doubt.

They had no warning except for the two or three seconds of footsteps sounding on the parquet floor from the top of the stairs to the bedroom.

She sat up instantly, the blood draining from her face. He hadn't moved from lying on his side, and remained there stock-still. A fug of passing wind went unnoticed.

He'd recall the image later in graphic detail, and everything that followed. A writer could not gloss over the full scenario with the cliché of 'what happened next was a blur'. Far from it! In Andrew's mind, a painter might have stilled the original scene, capturing it with great effect: a man framed by the doorway with a look of bewilderment, a stricken woman sitting up in bed and pulling the bed sheet up to cover her flushed breasts as if decorum required it, and a man climbing from the bed, his genitals concealed by the profile of a naked thigh that looked bone-white in the drench of moonlight. Except for the man's thigh in the foreground, all in sombre light like a Rembrandt.

The image lived on for Andrew. The action rushed forward. Malcolm charged. Andrew, climbing from the bed, was at a disadvantage, and his nakedness gave him little defence. They grappled before Andrew could reach for his clothes on the floor and make a quick getaway.

For a few seconds, Malcolm had cursed, but when he reached Andrew, he began to hit out wildly. Andrew shielded himself as best he could, and didn't retaliate, but tried to hug his attacker to pin the flailing fists. He'd wronged this man enough.

For half a minute they continued this grotesque dance around the room until Malcolm, without the use of his arms, managed to knee him in the groin. Before bending over in pain, Andrew pushed his assailant hard, and Malcolm, reeling backwards, fell over a pouffe near the dressing table, landing on his back.

Still in excruciating pain, Andrew retrieved his clothes and shoes and headed for the door. Fortunately, Malcolm had fallen on the other side of the room and offered no further resistance.

'You bastard, you filthy rotten bastard!' shrilled from the other side of the room, and stopped Andrew in his flight for an instant.

He hadn't been mistaken. The blasphemy was not Malcolm's. It was Cindy's. His last look revealed the two of them sitting and rocking on the carpet, holding and consoling each other in an empathy of tears.

Its Own Reward

She craned forward so that her face almost touched the mirror, smoothing an eyebrow with a moistened fingertip before withdrawing a pace to examine herself more critically. It was just as well it was no longer the fashion to have lips that were pillar-box-red, carmine or hibiscus tangerine. It wouldn't have suited her complexion at all. Better her more subdued mulberry.

Jamie was wearing a cotton dress in sunflower yellow with buttons up the front. Is it too fitting, she wondered, concerned that it might make her breasts too conspicuous.

Am I pretty, she asked herself, staring into the hazel eyes and tossing back her shoulder-length blonde hair. No one, apart from her mother, had ever told her so. She pirouetted so that her dress swirled around her knees, lifted by the motion. Felt foolish. Afraid someone might see her pretence. Left the question unanswered.

Apart from her school uniform for a posh private girls' school, she'd only had one party dress in her adolescent years that had to make do for the endless run of birthdays in the mansions of her eastern suburbs friends. Although the girls were kind, and made no comment, her less privileged position was inescapable, and her mother, who she loved dearly, somehow found a way to buy the necessary presents.

'Less privileged' did not mean poor. The family had moved from the country, where they'd worked a cattle farm and where the children attended a little school staffed by nuns. Jamie had four brothers and two sisters. She was the middle child of seven, and as her mother worked, and her three elder brothers went to boarding school, she was often cast in the role of additional mother, and on the odd occasions that her mother had work commitments that took her away, surrogate mother.

Even at the age of nine, that meant changing the nappies of Ted, her younger brother, sometimes ensuring that her other younger siblings arrived safely at school, and helping to feed the remainder of the family. She shared a bedroom with Irene, a younger sister who talked incessantly, oblivious to her study demands. Her older sister Kay was a blooming adolescent, then and thereafter a law unto herself, and when entrusted with looking after her siblings when the parents needed a rare weekend away, disappeared, cautioning Jamie to keep her secret from their parents. This meant the responsibility fell to Jamie, but she didn't complain and never let on.

The situation didn't improve with her maturing years. Her mother was diagnosed with cancer, and although she lived well into Jamie's womanhood, it created further strain as she tried to help her mother in any way she could. Her mother was her best friend and ally, and even when she died, Jamie never stopped dreaming of their imagined phone calls, sometimes waking in the night and calling her name. By this time, Kay was married, and her brothers were either at university, or living away from home.

Was it the face of a twenty five-year-old looking back reflectively from the mirror? Smooth. Open. Not unattractive. Did it bear the imprint of innocence? And was hers the body of a mature woman? A girl who'd come of age. She ran her open hands down her sides, testing the curve from her waist to her hips. One of her brothers had baited her years ago by telling her she was fat. Do people not know how long a hurtful remark, even if given in the non-discerning childhood years, can carry its sting? She didn't react, and wouldn't remind him now. He'd be mortified.

Has life passed me by, she wondered. Do I look like a little girl in my button-up dress? She'd certainly never had any of Kay's sophistication.

*

'He's really nice,' she told Kris when they met for coffee. Kris was the one school friend with whom she'd kept in close contact, and her meeting with Ruben was certainly worth reporting. She couldn't wait to do so.

Ruben was the brother of another girlfriend, one with whom she'd lost contact, but had sent a card to when hearing she was unwell. She visited when hearing of her friend's despondency, taking glacé fruit, and had met Ruben, who was attentive to her throughout her visit.

'I don't know how he got my number,' she told Kris. 'He must have asked around.' She told Kris of how the relationship began, the frisson of their first meeting alone, and the romance she assumed would last forever.

Kris was pleased for her friend. It was Jamie's very naivety that was appealing, a quality of unworldliness that made her different from some of the would-be sophisticates she knew. She was without pretence. She was without malice. She may even, Kris thought, be without reasonable expectations. She'd never had a serious boyfriend. She'd been busy studying, teaching and looking after her family. And Kris was very aware it was a profile of the potentially vulnerable, a profile that needed to be changed for her own benefit, or at least tinkered with around the edges, before it was the source of a greater hurt.

'Owen and I have worked out a democratic way of making our relationship work,' Kris said. Owen had been her boyfriend for the last year, and the explanation she intended to provide for Jamie was her advice for ensuring equity for beginning romances. Perhaps a way of helping Jamie emerge from the constraints of her existing profile. 'We take turns in everything,' she began, 'with driving, with paying, though he sometimes pays a little more as he earns more. I'll only cook occasionally, and expect to be taken out regularly. I tell him when.'

Kris didn't want to be too explicit, and she didn't want to sound patronising, yet considered shifting the so-called equity in favour of the woman was a way of giving Jamie greater pause for thought. But she didn't want to be seen as a battleaxe. 'I like flowers and little gifts, token gifts, they don't have to be expensive…' She paused to consider what to say next.

Jamie was uneasy. Surely guidelines like these subtracted from the spontaneity of giving, made relationships into a checklist of obligations. She wanted to give, irrespective of whether she received. It's all she knew. If two people loved each other, she reasoned, they would want to give. You couldn't hold them back!

'Remember Berice.' Kris, thinking she might have said too much already, changed her tack. 'You remembered every birthday for years. You sent her money, you gave her that beautiful dressing gown when she was sick. You sent her daughter that doll for Christmas. Sure, she texted her thanks, but did she send you any present? Did she ever remember your birthday?'

Jamie wanted to say, 'That's not the point.' Instead she said nothing.

'Don't look so down,' Kris appeased, and took Jamie's hand across the table, stroking it. 'You're the best friend I've ever had.' A tear appeared and was quickly wiped away. 'I'm not trying to be mean. I know you can't change who you really are. It's just that I don't want Ruben, or any one, and that includes me, taking advantage of you. It's because I care.'

Jamie thanked her as they left the café and, because her friend still seemed to be emotional, embraced her before they parted.

'Let me know of any developments with Ruben,' Kris called from across the street with assumed cheerfulness. 'Promise.'

'Promise. I'll tell you my innermost secrets,' Jamie called back playfully.

They both laughed.

*

Their first meeting was at Brooklyn, a small town on the Hawkesbury River that catered mainly to tourists with ferry trips, walks along the foreshore, and grassy picnic grounds at the top of easily accessible cliffs. There was a marina, and eating places that catered to a variety of tastes. It became a sentimental retreat, a place to which they frequently returned.

Romance budded with the springtime flowers, and so did the aphrodisiac of talk and touch. It was approaching dusk when they left. The river was still, a glassy grey-blue, and an orange sun bathed the hilltop where they sat in an apricot wash, giving their faces a coppery sheen.

Over the following weeks, the dance of love with its incremental give and take closed in on intimacy, though Ruben was impressed by Jamie's restraint, a mark of how she perceived herself.

He already knew of her consideration for others. His sister was one such instance, and the more he thought of that first meeting, the more he felt that fate had been generous. He also knew that an expansive spirit sometimes comes at a cost, that people are more envious of simple goodness than they are of appearances, image, money or power, because it's a threat to the darkness that lurks inside them. Goodness cannot be bought or traded. It's non-negotiable.

Very early in the relationship, he knew of Jamie's concern for the well-being of her family, and her practice of sending cards or gifts, even to people she barely knew who had fallen ill or were depressed. She continued to do so even when the favour was not returned.

Ruben's family was delighted with the match, and were all very fond of Jamie. In retrospect, Ruben thought it was fortunate that she had received his mother's blessing, because she died suddenly of a stroke. Ruben was devastated and craved Jamie's near-constant presence as he indulged the incantation of bereavement. For the next few months, sitting with Jamie in their various haunts, he'd recall the images of his mother's love that salved the bloodied knees of infant boys, and grown men, and the family parlour games with the scent of gardenias beyond the family room window.

Jamie was a source of comfort for both Ruben and the other

members of the family and, as Ruben's sister was still unwell, undertook the task of organising the wake.

Ruben spoke haltingly at the funeral and, to Jamie's surprise, included her indirectly in his mother's eulogy, claiming that he'd only ever known two people who placed others' needs above their own. One, he said, was his mother and, while he didn't name the other, he looked at her, and many heads turned in her direction. They knew.

She didn't mention it afterwards, feeling that it might be calling for a restatement of the compliment. Fishing for praise. But Ruben did.

'You did so much,' he said, 'organising all that food, and when I saw you running around with the party pies and all those cups of tea…'

He was too emotional to continue, and they sat silently for a few minutes, hand in hand before he resumed.

'I sometimes wonder,' he said, 'whether helping people as much as my mother did,' and he turned to look directly at her, 'whether serving others like that, thinking that everyone else is more important…is really friend or foe.'

The words seem to hang in the air.

'But who am I?' he said after a long pause, 'to make judgements like that.'

The planned five-day trip to a rented house in Hawks Nest was a strategy organised by three male friends to help him overcome his post-funeral depression and lethargy. He was grateful for the support, excited by the prospect of male bonding, and apologetic to Jamie as it clashed with the date she'd organised for Ruben to meet her parents who were now in semi-retirement and lived three hundred kilometres away.

'Are you sure you don't mind?' he asked.

'I can organise another time for you to meet Mum and Dad,' she replied, concealing her disappointment. 'Your friends have taken this time off work, so it wouldn't be fair on them.'

'You're sure,' Ruben rechecked, sensing her disappointment, yet hoping she wouldn't change her mind.

She made three large casseroles for them, pork, pineapple beef and a chicken curry. 'My brothers used to eat like horses,' she said. 'I hope the boys like them,' and she waved the panel van with its whooping passengers goodbye with an empty heart.

She missed Ruben for those five days. It was their first prolonged absence from each other, and she considered it a test of their feeling. That at least was an effective way of coping with the loss, and giving it meaning.

'They say absence makes the heart…' were his first words after he'd returned and they'd hugged on her doorstep, and seeing her nodding, there was no need to complete the proverb.

*

Six weeks later, Kris talked Jamie into accompanying her for a long weekend to Fremantle, where her favourite aunt lived. Ruben was to be away on a mandatory professional development course for his work, and didn't mind her going. Jamie was excited. She had done very little travel, and even the plane trip was anticipated with enthusiasm.

Jamie liked the aunt, and the three of them spent the reminder of the first day shopping, sampling restaurants and visiting the old world charm of Fremantle.

On the second day, they decided to take the boat the eighteen kilometres to Rottnest Island and see the quokkas. As the boat was about to depart, Owen came running along the wharf, calling out to the ferryman, and boarding the boat as it was pulling away.

Kris was taken by surprise. This wasn't planned. A spur of the moment decision, he told Kris breathlessly. They hugged, delighted to see each other, and when they reached the island, Owen made it clear that he would like to be alone with his girlfriend. Kris opened her hands in a supplicating gesture to Jamie, mouthed 'Sorry', and hurried away, towed by Owen.

Jamie walked aimlessly around the island, with the excitement of visiting the snorkelling destinations and seeing the coral and tropical fish quickly evaporating now that she was alone. She had coffee and lunch at different cafés, and visited two beaches, but she didn't swim as she and Kris had planned. And she didn't change into her costume. She watched the waves lapping the shore, the picnicking families, the squawking antics of the gulls and the small children making sand castles.

She met Kris later that day on the return boat, clinging to Owen, and felt more than ever the interloper.

'You'll never guess,' Kris told her excitedly. 'He proposed.'

Jamie was pleased for her friend, and the news was greeted with great excitement when they all returned to the aunt's place in Fremantle. Plans were discussed, there were phone calls to home, and loud laughter. Jamie found it difficult to contribute. Kris looked in her direction a couple of times with what might have been concern, before her festive mood returned almost immediately.

Jamie caught the same plane back as the betrothed couple, but wasn't able to sit with them. She arrived home spiritless. It wasn't the time she'd hoped it would be.

*

The sharing of a bereavement with its need for regeneration, and Ruben's brief absence, brought them closer together, and over the next month they shared happy times going to the beach, visiting the nearby recreation spots, or simply eating together and watching television.

They had a romantic long weekend at the Hunter Valley, where they discussed a long-term future, and started what became a personal culture from verbal nonsense, fun for them if incomprehensible to others.

During these months there were several incidents of Jamie becoming disappointed at people's failure to even acknowledge what she had done for them, her work colleagues, her family and her friends.

Her young brother Ted whose bottom she had wiped when she was only nine, still regarded her as a surrogate mother, even though he was now a man and had left home years before. He called on her to run errands, and drive him to the airport. He even invited himself to dinner. Her sister Kay, now a mother of two young children, had unrealistic expectations of Aunt Jamie's child-minding responsibilities.

Colleagues at the school, rewarded her competence, and disguised their own incompetence or laziness, by devolving as much of their work to her as might be seen to be reasonable. Jamie assumed the extra load with good grace.

Ruben thought she failed to understand that the more she did for people, the more they would expect from her. He began to see her goodness, or naivete, as her own need, and a rod for her own back.

He told her so, and while she acknowledged the wisdom of what he said, she argued that she was no fool, she did know what people were like, they weren't all inconsiderate, and she'd continue trying to make a difference by being kind, requited or not. And she'd still refuse to retaliate when someone had been demonstrably unkind.

'It's who I am, Ruben,' she said almost regrettably, and then more assuredly, 'I know I'm not worldly, and I know I can't change. I've thought about what it would be like to do so, even tried to ignore needs crying out to be met, and I've come to realise that I have to be true to myself.'

There was no real conflict for Jamie. She certainly felt discouraged at times by someone's lack of consideration, but real disappointment was when a gesture by her, meant to meet an obvious need, was not even acknowledged. Her actions were never calculated, at least not in terms of expecting more than nominal appreciation.

In the face of comments like these, Ruben's criticism of her un-worldliness would collapse, and he'd tell her how lucky he was to have met her, praise her for being so selfless and tell her of his love.

He could sympathise with Jamie, regarding himself as more considerate, and more responsive to people's needs than most, and believing that self-sacrifice was called for on occasions, but he drew the line at putting others first all the time. That was a denial of your own worth.

He sometimes experienced uneasiness, even guilt, thinking he'd been unkind to her when he'd been critical of her 'blind' giving, even wondered if she were more magnanimous than him, if her goodness was something he could never attain.

The years had taught him that conflict was a part of what it means to love someone, and while his relationship with Jamie was a feeling more powerful than he'd ever experienced before, there were also dark moments when its heights were impossible to sustain, and it plunged to depths of imagined affront before the pain of friction spurred them to renewal.

*

Their friends and families saw them as the ideal couple, suited in every way, and could only speculate as to why the relationship failed. They were saddened by it. Jamie and Ruben would both be repeatedly asked why, and even though the passion behind the reasons often weakens with each revisiting over the weeks and months, the answers Jamie and Ruben gave never varied.

Ruben was aware that the usual tactic is the need to justify, to provide a litany of reasons as if the world requires an answer, and if the split is bitter, a list of grievances. The items on such lists are always in constant flux. Time and emotion reorders the reasons, adds and subtracts.

And it's assumed that the reasons can be articulated, that each person involved can tease them out in some reasonable way. But do people always know why? Any relationship is a complex dynamic. Is there such a thing as a science of separation?

These concerns of Ruben's were why he refused to provide an account, though he might have provided some of the issues he'd raised with Jamie. It was no one else's business anyway. 'Does there have to be a reason,' he'd say, or 'Some relationships just end, they fade away.'

It wasn't long before people stopped asking.

Kris assumed the role of Jamie's principal interrogator. 'Was it you or him who ended it?' she asked boldly, having heard that Ruben had been seen with another woman.

Of course rumours were always rife at a time like this, and for all anyone knew, it might have been his sister.

Jamie didn't answer. Perhaps she hadn't heard.

'Why did it end?' Kris inquired less acidly, convinced that her friend was blameless, and realising that hostility was not the way forward, not if she wanted Jamie to open up.

'Ruben did nothing wrong,' she replied as her eyes filled with tears. 'It was all my fault.'

Life's Ironies

At the age of sixty-seven, the claims of mortality begin to press more insistently. It's irony perhaps that they're also keenly felt at fifteen in the throes of adolescence when we realise that what we believed to be certainties in our lives are transitory, even life itself. Reading Keats or Thomas Gray at school probably furthers this understanding.

But at sixty-seven, the changes are not those signifying growth, emergence into the exciting freedom of living, like those in adolescence, but rather those signifying decline.

So each morning I'd abdicate my bed that claimed me like a jealous lover, open the curtains on a world that marks the time indelibly with season's march, adjust my eyes to the light, comb my fingers through my thinning hair and prepare for the day ahead. There were times I'd walk purposefully into a room and wonder why. Sometimes I'd see my long- dead father's face in the bathroom mirror with a gently mocking smile, and wonder if we grow more like ourself or those who've gone before.

Even at sixty, sex and sport take a grudging second place to politics and medicine, the former bearing on the likelihood of comfort in our maturing years, and the latter an unwelcome reminder of our impermanence, the shared stories coloured with each repetition, and meeting with incredulity. 'Remember Neville Duff at school, sat behind Keith Hall, prostate cancer, died last year, and of course the lovely Jenny, not doing too well at all, a few months at best.'

School reunions were an acid test. The list of truants increased. The names of the departed were read out by a member of the organising committee, and their exploits lamely venerated. There was always someone I didn't know and had to draw on my fading mental map of classroom seating for a clue.

Some of my former classmates were older versions of what I remembered. Others were not recognisable. In some, the lines bit deep in faces, bellies swelled, and liver spots spread like measles. Though to be fair, some were remarkably well preserved.

In our school years, we'd dismiss 'the old' as if they were another species, the 'use-by' date long passed. We all saw Miss Hemming, the French teacher as old, but she was probably only in her mid-thirties. 'Old' meant 'adult' or, for some, 'not groovy'.

My name's Peter Allthorpe. At sixty-seven, I counted myself lucky. Life's roulette had given me two reasonably health-free and long-living parents. As the eternal romantic, and inspired by some medieval ideal, I had exercised regularly from my teenage years, and still played a number of sports. I assumed that this with my beyond school studies as a young man, and my creative efforts more recently in my retirement, were a hedge against the darker challenges of age.

I lived with my wife Ellie in a home we'd bought as a young married couple. At sixty-seven, our birthdays a month apart, we'd been married for forty-two years, and I have no hesitation in saying 'happily'. She was my spouse and closest friend. The children had their own grown families. Ellie didn't share my passion for keeping fit, but a slim build and correct eating ensured her good health.

My annual medical revealed some 'anomalies' requiring further blood tests. I was disturbed by the word and its lack of precision. It meant an aberration or an irregularity. In other words, something didn't make sense. My GP, quite correctly, didn't or couldn't shed any light, beyond saying that it was quite common for tests of this sort to involve follow-ups. Besides, she didn't want to hazard a guess.

*

I sat alone in the waiting room of Mr Enright. Specialists apparently prefer 'Mister' to 'Doctor'. Ellie had wanted to come for moral support and because she was worried, but I downplayed its significance, and said I'd prefer to go alone. I wished then I hadn't. I began to think the worst.

There was a fish tank in the waiting room, supposedly to calm the nerves of patients, and I watched the rounded mouthing of the fish that glided with goitred eyes among the swaying ferns in their silent phosphorescent existence. At that moment, I thought my world felt remarkably like theirs.

I listened for sounds behind the door, beyond the wadded stillness of the waiting room. There were none. I was sitting beside a cheerless spray of tenth-real flannel flowers, thumbing the scoops from dated magazines on sex romps, tired romance and pregnancies. A woman sat opposite behind a vacant face scourged to would-be rosy health, with a khaki envelope of unopened scans on her lap.

'Are you OK?' I asked her, surprised that it was my voice we heard. It sounded as if it came from the depths of the fish tank, yet it drew a nod and silent thanks.

'Mr Allthorpe.' The door opened, and the specious safety of uncertainty was gone.

Mr Enright was younger than I had expected, dressed in suit and tie, balding, and with a gentle manner that inspired immediate confidence. He motioned to a leather chair, and swivelled his own to face me. 'There were some anomalies in the blood test,' he said softly. That word again. He asked me to remove my shirt and felt around my neck and abdomen with cold fingers. 'Have you had any fever?'

I shook my head as alarm grew.

'Any fatigue, loss of appetite and weight, any unusual night sweating, any swelling in the glands?'

'I'm tireder now,' I said with a lame attempt at humour, 'but I am in my late sixties. Otherwise no.' I said this more emphatically as if I needed to dismiss his suspicions.

He seemed a little surprised and stopped the examination. 'I'd like you to have an MRI scan.'

The woman with the unopened envelope of scans, the only other patient, was looking even more anxious as Enright shook my hand at the door, and moved across to whisper to the receptionist to arrange the next appointment. I wondered if their talk needed to be subdued in the interests of patient sanity.

A fortnight later, after a scan and additional blood test, I was in his rooms again. I was worried, but told Ellie the tests had been 'regulation', that Enright was known to be particularly thorough, and there was no need for her to come. Of course she protested.

'Peter,' and with his use of first names, I was instantly on guard. We'd only met once before. 'It's not the best of news, I'm afraid. It's non-Hodgkin's lymphoma. Stage four.'

I knew what stage four meant. Composed at first, I asked what needed to be asked, my calm as heavy as a summer doona that needed to be thrown aside. He answered, his voice droning years away, a blowfly circling on the light, while I floated beyond myself as if I wasn't the sole agenda after all.

'How long?' I asked when I sensed a pause in his monologue detailing the required treatment.

'About twelve months,' Enright answered. Perhaps twelve months was meant to sound better than one year. Strength in numbers. 'Of course,' he hastened to add, 'one never knows. There's a lot we can do now. New treatments are introduced all the time. New medicines.' He stopped short of saying miracles happen.

I remember needing Ellie as I'd never needed her before. She'd have asked the questions I later regretted not having asked. She'd have made it clear then and there that it was something that had happened to both of us, and that we'd deal with it together.

Through the soft linoleum corridors, muting more than my tread, and out into the glare of summer's day, my shock was mantled by a show of common sense, my fleeting paranoia softened by nobility. I'll do this well, I thought. I'll make my death the crowning glory of my life.

Of course, such nobility would be sorely tested.

*

How a person copes with their own imminent death probably depends on how they perceive the purpose of life. Those who see all life, physical and spiritual, ending with death, may readily accept the void, or rail against it. Those who have a faith or believe in a life beyond death may find some comfort in that belief.

I believed in a God who controlled my destiny, and believed in the scriptural claims that the will of God is incomprehensible to we mortals. Knowing there was a purpose, even if I'd never know what it was, did provide some comfort, though I was still fearful of what Flaubert called the sudden irruption into nothingness.

Ellie was magnificent, never uttering a negative word and refusing to give up hope, even though we both knew her hight spirits were for my benefit. She was sometimes over-attentive, unwittingly robbing me of my needed opportunity to stay active, to feel I was still making a contribution. I feared being an invalid, and even more so being treated as one.

I'd never felt better, my current feeling of well-being belying the prognosis, but knew and feared the not-so-distant time when I might not be able to help myself and would be dependent on others.

There were many nights in that first month when sleep eluded me and painted my perceptions black, when demons nested in my overactive mind, and holograms of dozens of the already departed, parents, relatives and friends, appeared like ghost-train visions, one melting into another in an endless procession.

Some nights when I foolishly thought Ellie was asleep, I'd escape barefoot to the patio, grateful for the ice of quarry tiles, and suck great gulps of air, the hunger for a life that couldn't be stored for rainy days. And I'd search the bush in the sentient black beyond the house, in the belief that someone might be there with trumping rights to overturn this mortal trick, and listen to my silent plea implore a sleeping world. Those nights would usually end with the sudden feeling of Ellie's arm around my shoulders, and her head resting in the hollow of my neck as we stood facing the garden, before we climbed the stairs wordlessly together to attempt sleep once again.

Ellie did come with me in my first visit for treatment at Andrew Chang's, the oncologist. It was to be weeks, possibly months of chemotherapy. And there was the likelihood of radiotherapy after that. I thought of it as a downward spiral, the beginning of a process with an inevitable conclusion. Ellie saw it as the start of a process of hope, gave never-ending encouragement, and diverted me with joking references to the blossoming romances reported in the waiting room magazines. There was no fish tank, but there was help-yourself coffee and tea, and a two-thousand-piece jigsaw puzzle half finished on a table, to which all patients could contribute. Perhaps the painstaking effort needed served to remind us of our own need for patience.

*

A month or so after the diagnosis, the two girls arrived, Caroline with her husband from Sweden, and Claire, still single, from Western Australia.

'I'll stay as long as you need me,' Claire said, and realising the implications of her comment and the limited duration of my need, began to cry.

'I only have about ten days this time, Dad,' Caroline apologised, 'but I'll try to get back again a little later in the year.' She too was fragile.

Ellie made sure that there were no morbid moments between us. We went on picnics on the good days when the weekly chemo had lost its bite, we recalled good times and laughed around the dinner table, and we pored over photos of the girls as children and teenagers. I was grateful for this sharing time, but just occasionally, the better these times were, the harder it was to cast off the knowledge that they were coming to an end.

Caroline hugged me for a long time before she left, not wanting to let go in case I saw her tears. We were both wondering if we'd see each other again. Enright had said twelve months, but that was at best an approximation. What if it was only six or nine?

When Claire had gone, I threw myself into organising the details necessary for the futures of Ellie and the girls. Sitting around and moping could only lead to despair and feeling sorry for myself. I made some changes to my will, and visited my money manager.

'You've been a valued client for years, Peter,' he said emotionally. 'We'll make sure your family will always be comfortable.'

A month became two then three. It all seemed so unreal, particularly as I was still feeling quite well. Of course I looked at the literature to understand my likely progress, not only that dealing with my particular cancer, but the sequence of general coping from anger and resentment to final acceptance. I arrived quickly at the latter with very little of the former. I was well aware that the world did not operate on a principle of poetic justice. Besides, I'd been more fortunate than most. I'd had a good life.

*

After the sixth month, I returned to Andrew Chang for my regular visit after the usual round of blood tests. I was very familiar with his waiting room and office now. I was 'Peter' to Kelly, the blonde receptionist with whom I shared light-hearted banter, and went directly to the patient's chair in his office without his bidding.

'I have some shocking news, Peter,' he said. 'No, let me rephrase that. I have some extraordinary news.' He paused, I think to savour the moment. 'Sometimes in the medical world, there are things that can't be explained. It isn't an exact science.'

Just get on with it, I thought, and he saw me leaning forward expectantly on the chair.

'The cancer's gone,' he said. 'Not a trace.'

I stared at him in shock. It was like telling the ancients that the world was round. My imminent death was the foundation my life had been built on for the last half year. So it wasn't instant delight. Sometimes emotion lags behind knowledge.

'It's over then,' I eventually managed, still bewildered, the realisation slowly gathering force. I didn't know whether to laugh or cry.

'Obviously we'll need to see you again, say in two or three months, just to check,' and he came towards me, taking my hand in both of his. 'I can't tell you how pleased I am. There aren't that many good luck stories in my line of work.'

'Well, what was the count this time?' Ellie was waiting at the door when I arrived home, maintaining her cheerful presence.

And when I told her my news, she began to jump up and down, and dance around the front room, whooping and laughing. She rang Claire, and woke Caroline in the early hours in Sweden. She was all for a celebratory dinner, but I wanted a quiet night at home. I needed to consider this in the larger scheme of things.

A week later, Ellie had a heart attack in the kitchen. I rode with her in the ambulance to the hospital as she lapsed in and out of consciousness. Even with the pain, she managed a weak smile and squeezed my hand.

'We'll see it through together,' I said, ever mindful that it was the message she had so often given me.

There was a fainter squeeze of my hand and her eyes closed.

She was given a private room after two doctors had conducted thorough examinations.

'It's not good,' one told me in a very businesslike way. 'I'm afraid significant damage has been done.'

I sat in her room, reassuring her as she had been doing for me, until she lapsed into a coma.

'You need to prepare yourself, Mr Allthorpe,' the second doctor said more sympathetically. 'If there's anything you need to ask…'

For the rest of the day, I was in a daze, sitting bedside or occasionally walking the corridors for a coffee break. I rang the girls, who said they'd come immediately. The situation was difficult to grasp, and in my irrational frame of mind, I entertained the idea that one of us had been chosen, and because I'd been spared, because I'd cheated death, it had to be her.

What did 'prepare yourself' mean? Surely there was only one thing it could mean. I found myself mulling over a semantic analysis. 'You need to.' Not 'you might', or 'perhaps you could consider.' 'Need' carried a finality.

They say the comatose can hear your every word. Nurses tell you to profess your love, seek absolution, tell them you'll be fine or, if you're so inclined, pray. And so I spoke to Ellie, recalling the good times, saying how lucky I was to have her, telling her that I still needed her and not to go anywhere. Sometimes I was light-hearted and laughed. At other times I was anguished, my tears flowing like hers had for me. Occasionally I'd lean over and kiss her forehead, avoiding the breathing tubes.

The nursing staff made me a makeshift couch in her room so that we could spend the night together. I'd watch the calmness of her face, and listen to her stertorous breath rasp life from laden air.

My earlier endless chatter to her revived odd images, her raiding the box of Turkish delight and strenuously denying it laughing as she did so, the way she'd bite her lip when curious or absorbed, her gambolling about when excited, the hilarious posturing when she addressed a drive from the tee in golf, and the endless tokens and novel ways she'd come up with of expressing her love.

At two-thirty a.m. the grating sound stopped and a palpable stillness filled the room. Whenever people later spoke of the spirit moving, this was the moment I'd remember. I knew there was no need to press buzzers or call for help. There was no hurry. I've often tried to recall the exact nature of my feelings at that moment. I think it was a profound emptiness. She was at peace now, and I didn't want to leave her. These were precious moments as she prepared for a final journey. I was a jealous lover, resentful of being disturbed.

It must have been two hours later that I kissed her one final time, and after lingering at the door, still reluctant to leave, approached the nurses' station to interrupt their chatter. I didn't say a word. One look at me and they knew. One of them went to Ellie to confirm and returned to nod. They very gently explained the procedure the hospital would follow, and one of them escorted me to the front doors, placing a hand on my arm as a gesture of sympathy.

My drive away was metaphor, consigning present loss to mellow past, advancing by retreat. The world was still asleep, the darkness of the streets blushed by amber stars, and Ellie was everywhere, the brief ubiquity that's granted when you kiss the cheek of time.

'Don't leave me,' I said aloud. 'Not yet.'

As the car moved noiselessly on empty roads, our dialogue was loving and pure, and while I was sore at heart, we were at peace, not raging against the dying of the light.

*

I've just turned ninety-three, and all I've been telling you happened twenty-five years ago. If you think it's not a very uplifting story, you're wrong. Of course I miss Ellie. Not a day goes by when I don't talk with her, or give silent thanks for the many wonderful years we shared together. It might sound corny, the pabulum of the cheap magazines in Enright's and Wong's waiting rooms, but in a very real sense our love lives on.

If you think such a sequence of events must call into question the place of God or a much bigger picture of the meaning of the universe in my life, you'd be wrong again. Why should a larger meaning or a divine purpose conform to our own minuscule wants?

I clung to life all those years ago. Now death has no sting. Surely all of life is a preparation for death. If well lived, perhaps we have no need or right to cling on to it. I accept my part in the cycle of life and death, the grand plan, and am grateful for it.

Claire lives with me now, and we do our best to help each other in any way we can. I look after the money matters, and do some of the domestic chores. And I still have sufficient mobility to get to the supermarket once a week. It has become an important outing, releasing me from a regime of reading and writing, to rub shoulders with the real world.

There's rarely a time I don't hear a couple of women, typically in their fifties, lamenting the onslaught of age, talking of the pigment marks on their legs, the arthritis, the way some of the body drops or sags, and sharing the ricocheting stories of early bereavements.

I just smile.